Guns at Rimrock Creek

Piers Lomax was a tough *hombre,* but straight as a die. He had built up the Horseshoe ranch, which was the largest in Rimrock, and now he was dead, apparently killed in a riding incident. His beautiful but wild daughter Sabina was in charge of the ranch, but she had fallen for the unscrupulous Reece Berry, who was determined to fire most of Lomax's cowboys and bring in his own gunslingers.

Amongst those dismissed was Matt Flint, Lomax's loyal foreman, and now he was roped in to try and prevent a range war. He was deadly with a gun, but almost single-handed had to fight the ruthless land-grabbers led by Reece Berry.

His life was on the line and he faced death at every turn. Was he brave and skilful enough to buck the odds?

Guns at Rimrock Creek

DAVID SOMERS

A Black Horse Western

ROBERT HALE · LONDON

© Sydney J. Bounds 1954
This edition 2002

ISBN 0 7090 7170 1

Robert Hale Limited
Clerkenwell House
Clerkenwell Green
London EC1R 0HT

Typeset by
Derek Doyle & Associates, Liverpool.
Printed and bound in Great Britain by
Antony Rowe Limited, Wiltshire.

1
BAD NEWS

From the pine-flanked bluffs above the river, Matthew Flint could look down on the cluster of frame buildings that made up the town of Rimrock. He halted a moment, a big-boned man with grey eyes and darkish hair, and watched the light of the evening sun reflect on the few windows fitted with glass. It looked quiet enough; in a couple of hours, riders would come in from the ranges, lamps would go on in the saloons, and the town would liven up.

His gaze shifted from the grey huddle of huts, to the silvered river winding across the plains. He stared across open rangeland to the mountains on the distant horizon and knew a feeling of pride. He was looking at Horseshoe country, and Flint was foreman of the Horseshoe.

Piers Lomax, Flint's boss, had built up a big spread, the biggest in these parts. There were

other ranges, the Lazy S, Storey's, Buchan's
Double U, Webb's outfit; but these could only be
compared to the Horseshoe empire when considered collectively. The Horseshoe was the real
power in Rimrock.

Flint nudged his horse, a big bay roan, to
motion and continued down the trail. There was
dust on his broad-brimmed stetson and on his
high-heeled boots; his shirt was soiled with
sweat from the three-days' ride and his square
jaw had a dark stubble. He was a solid, slow-
moving man, proud of the part he had played in
making the Horseshoe one of the biggest ranches
in the west.

The roan jogged on steadily, not a handsome
beast to took at, but an animal with staying
power; horse and rider had this quality in
common. Flint frowned then suddenly, thinking;
Lomax wasn't going to be pleased when his foreman reported time wasted. He had ridden to Blue
Rocks to buy cattle rumoured for sale – but the
rumour had come too late and the herd had been
sold off twenty-four hours before Flint arrived.

The trail levelled off and a straggly wire fence
indicated he was near the town. Ahead, the buildings sprawled out either side of the dirt track. He
saw figures moving about, forming a crowd, and
heard voices raised; Rimrock was not as quiet as
he'd thought atop the bluff. He set the roan at a
canter and entered the town.

He came up behind the crowd, swung out of the saddle and hitched his roan to the rail in front of Dobie's saloon. Backs were towards him and the crowd was making too much noise to notice one lone rider coming in with the sun behind him. Someone was calling, 'Quiet, quiet – let's talk this thing out.' Flint heard a reference to the Horseshoe, but he missed the gist of the remark in the hubbub.

He looked over heads to the man standing on the boardwalk and calling for silence, and his brow furrowed when he recognized Ben Storey. Storey was small in size and mind, a man with petty ways; he had always been jealous of Piers Lomax, hating his success. If trouble was starting, Storey would be the man behind it.

A small voice at Flint's elbow said: 'Hello, Matt.'

Flint did not have to turn. He knew the voice – Nora's – but he did turn, because it always gave him pleasure to look on her. He said, his gaze taking in her slim build and trim riding suit, her chestnut curls and pretty face, 'Hello, Nora.'

He was quick to notice that she was not smiling, that the dancing light was absent from her eyes; and that meant big trouble.

Nora Hurst said, quietly: 'Matt; Lomax is dead.'

It jolted Flint. It hit him hard, but he did not question the girl's word; he knew her too well for that. Lomax dead – he thought what that could mean – the end even of Horseshoe, possibly. He

7

grunted, swinging round to watch Ben Storey, to listen to what the rancher had to say. With Lomax dead, Storey would be talking big.

Storey had managed to get silence from the crowd. He made a dark figure in his shabby black suiting, and his pasty face wore an expression of personal triumph. He raised a hand and spoke.

'This is our chance,' he said. 'Your chance. The chance to expand, grab more land and cattle, and make real money. Lomax always held us back. He took the best land and we had to put up with what was left. Well, Lomax is dead now . . .'

He paused a moment, looking at faces in the crowd, gauging the response to his words. He went on -

'Things are going to be different in Rimrock. Lomax is dead and a girl can't run an outfit the size of Horseshoe. You can guess what will happen – the ranch will break up. Well, we'll help it a little! We'll move in and take what we want. Take the land and move our cattle onto it. Take any cattle that drift on to our new spreads. We'll bust the Horseshoe wide open!'

Matthew Flint was very still, his gaze fixed on the small, dark figure of Ben Storey. He felt in his pocket, pulled out a briar pipe and pouch of tobacco, and, with slow, deliberate movements, rammed tobacco into the bowl of the pipe. His hands were large and seemed clumsy for this operation. He struck a match and held it over the

8

tobacco, sucking quietly. He waved away an excess of smoke and concentrated on Storey.

'We'll play it the way Lomax himself played it,' Storey said. 'Lomax never asked permission. He took what he wanted, and he had the men to back his play. Well, we'll take what we want – Horseshoe land!'

'You bet we will,' growled a large, thick-set man at the front of the crowd. 'The Horseshoe is finished and we're taking over.'

Flint recognized the speaker; Buchan, owner of the Double U – a bully who enjoyed throwing his weight around when he had no opposition. He and Storey made a fine pair.

Another man spoke, his voice cutting across the murmur of the crowd.

'A fine way to talk. Men – real men – planning to move in on a woman's land and take it from her. Not one of you would be talking this way if Lomax were here!'

That was Dan Hurst, Nora's father and boss of the Lazy S. He was a slim man, not tall, with grey in his hair. He was standing next to Rimrock's sheriff.

Buchan grunted: 'Shut yore trap, Hurst. Sabina's no good, and you know it.'

Sheriff Arnold drawled: 'Dan's right. You *hombres* are a mean lot – what's more, what you're planning is outside the law. Now, break it up and go home. The Horseshoe can look after itself.'

9

Ben Storey waved his fists and shouted: 'You've got no power now Lomax is dead, Arnold. He was the only man backing you in office – you're finished in Rimrock. We'll elect a new man, one who doesn't take orders from Horseshoe!'

'That's right,' Buchan growled. 'We've no use for you, Arnold, so pipe down.'

Flint pressed down the tobacco in his pipe with his thumb. A slow hatred for Storey was building up inside him. He thrust the briar into the corner of his mouth and hitched up his gunbelt.

Arnold didn't say any more. The sheriff was outnumbered, and knew it. Storey had the crowd with him – and Arnold wasn't a strong character. With Lomax behind him, his word had been law. On his own, he wouldn't take the risk of sticking his neck out.

Nora touched Flint's arm.

'It's no good, Matt,' she said. 'You can't fight all of them. Better leave it alone.'

Storey was talking again, wildly, swinging the crowd with him.

'You all know the sort of man Lomax was. He thought he owned Rimrock – we were just tolerated. Well, now's your chance to even the score. We're moving in and taking what we want, and there ain't no-one to stand against us!'

Flint pushed Nora to one side. 'Keep out of this,' he said briefly.

Someone in the crowd turned his head; Webb,

10

another of the small ranchers. Seeing Flint, he started, nudged his neighbour and passed the word.

'Matt Flint's here!'

A whisper ran through the crowd. The ranks parted, leaving an avenue leading straight from Flint to Ben Storey. The word reached Storey – 'Flint's here!' – and he faltered in his stride. His words died away, and, for a long moment, there was a hush.

Then Flint walked slowly and deliberately through the avenue of men, to stop in front of Ben Storey. He said, coldly: 'You're forgetting something, Ben. Horseshoe isn't finished while I'm foreman. Any of you *hombres* trying to move in on Horseshoe land will collect lead – my lead!'

Storey's face was deathly white. He licked his lips nervously. 'Maybe you haven't heard, Flint?' he said. 'Lomax is dead. That means—'

Flint snapped: 'Shut up! And come down off the boards, you've finished talking for today, Ben.'

Storey looked round wildly for help, but he had set himself up as spokesman, and the others were leaving it to him. He stepped down from the boardwalk, sliding round Flint.

'You're not worth hitting,' Matthew Flint said. He turned his gaze on Buchan. 'You were doing a lot of talking, Buchan – and you're more my size. D'yuh have any more to say?' Buchan went red in the face.

'You fool, Flint!' he snarled. 'The Horseshoe is finished. You can't bring back the dead.'

Flint balled his fist and raked his knuckles across Buchan's cheek.

'That's fighting talk,' he said. 'Put up yore fists – or back down!'

Buchan stared at him, then turned and pushed his way through the crowd. He had refused the challenge. Someone jeered, but Buchan kept going. He didn't look back. The crowd began to break up.

Flint said: 'The Horseshoe is still behind yuh, Sheriff!' Arnold drew his gun and stepped to the front.

'All right now,' he said quickly. 'This talk of lawlessness has got to stop. I don't want any more of it. Return to your homes, pronto.'

The men dispersed quietly, some moving for their horses, others entering the saloons. Sheriff Arnold said:

'Thanks, Matt. I wouldn't want you to think I was shunning my duty, but a mob is a nasty thing to handle. Thanks for helping out.'

Flint nodded curtly.

'Any time, Sheriff. You can rely on the Horseshoe to back the law.'

Arnold walked away, trying to appear unhurried. He went into his office and the door shut tight behind him. Flint smiled in a hard way. Nora and Dan Hurst joined him.

Hurst said: 'You handled that well, Matt, but don't think you've ended it. Soon as your back's turned, Storey and Buchan will be making trouble again.'

Flint knocked the dottle from his pipe and pushed the briar into his pocket.

'We'll see. Thanks for talking up for the Horseshoe, Dan. That took courage in front of a mob, and I won't forget it. I'll see that Sabina hears about it, too.'

Nora's eyes flashed at his mention of Sabina. 'What's going to happen now, Matt?' she asked. 'Will the Horseshoe break up?'

The question irritated Flint.

'How should I know?' he snapped back. 'Ask Sabina!' He steadied himself. 'Sorry, Nora, but I guess Lomax's death has upset me more than I knew. The Horseshoe will carry on if I have any say in the matter.'

Hurst shook his head doubtfully.

'It's going to mean trouble,' he said. 'I don't like it.' Flint got around to the question which had been bothering him.

'How did Lomax die?' Hurst shrugged.

'I don't know the whole story, Matt. Seems he took a fall from his horse and cracked his skull on a rock,'

Flint's lips tightened. Piers Lomax had been a real westerner, one of the old breed, a man who could ride before he walked.

13

It was asking a lot of any man to believe he'd been thrown by his mount.

Hurst saw the way he was thinking, and said: 'Storey wouldn't have the guts for it, Matt. He'll take advantage of Lomax's death, but he's not concerned in it.'

'So I'm to believe it was an accident?' Flint's tone had a sarcastic edge to it. 'That sticks in my throat, Dan.'

He let his eyes wander past Hurst and his daughter, taking in the length of Main Street with its saloons and frame shacks, the gaping windows and smokeless chimneys. His gaze rested on the bay roan tethered outside Dobie's, and he shifted his feet.

'Time for me to be moving,' he said. 'Tell me, how did Sabina take it?'

Hurst shrugged.

'I don't know, Matt. No one from Horseshoe's been into town. We only heard the news today.'

Flint said, harshly: 'Storey didn't waste much time!'

He raised his hat to Nora and moved for his horse. The girl followed him across the street and watched him mount. She held the roan's reins a moment, and said:

'This is going to change things for you, Matt. Remember, if things go bad on you, you're always welcome at the Lazy S. Dad would be glad to have you ride for him.'

14

'I'll remember,' Flint promised.

She stood back, and he urged the roan forward, picking up speed as he left the town behind him.

The sun was almost down, the plain streaked with a rich red glow, the distant mountains a majestic purple. Matthew Flint rode without seeing the beauty of the landscape; he lived in his thoughts and his mind was troubled.

Piers Lomax had been a good man, a hard man where his cattle empire was concerned, but straight and honest. It made Flint angry that Ben Storey should try to make him out a landgrabber, taking what he wanted by force. Lomax had won through because he worked hard and had taken a big view of things – and for that, Flint admired him.

What was going to happen to the Horseshoe now? That was the thought uppermost in Flint's mind. The ranch would go to Sabina, Lomax's daughter. Would she be big enough to run it the way her father had?

That there was going to be trouble, Flint did not doubt. Storey and Buchan were only stopped temporarily; they would seize on any weakness Sabina showed as an excuse to strike. It looked to Flint like range war was in the offing, and he had no liking for that. But Matt's duty lay with Horseshoe; long ago, he had promised Lomax he would stand by Sabina if anything should happen to the rancher. And that worried Flint, for he had never got on well with Sabina Lomax.

Flint rode on, covering the miles of scrub and grassland to the Horseshoe ranch at an easy pace. He stopped himself thinking about the future, for that lay in Sabina's hands – and he could not guess how she might act. Of one thing only was he sure – that he would respect Piers Lomax's wish and stand by her to the end.

2
SABINA LOMAX

Darkness pressed down like a heavy shroud as Flint reached the Horseshoe ranch. He rode into the patio and hitched his horse to the corral. Lights showed from the big house, a rough barn of a place, and from the punchers' bunkhouse. It was unnaturally quiet.

He walked towards the house, trying to marshal his thoughts into words, to prepare a speech of consolation for Sabina. The yellow glare of oil lamps pushed back the night shadows as far as the lone pine which dominated the patio. Lomax had left the one tree, tall and majestic, to give shade from the burning heat of summer; he had been fond of sitting under the tree of an evening, smoking, planning Horseshoe's future.

The dirt had been raked over at the foot of the tree; a small mound showed, and a wooden cross stuck up from the ground, straight and proud for all to see. Flint read the simple inscription which had been carved on the cross:

PIERS LOMAX

He removed his hat and stood silent before the grave, paying his final respects to a man he had admired, a great man, a pioneer of the west. Lomax would have liked it, if he could know he was buried in the shade of the lone pine. The thought flashed through Flint's head: They sure buried him quick!

He turned away as a man came from the bunkhouse, a man with a long jaw and both sadness and anxiety revealed in his face. It was Kincaid, one of the Horseshoe riders. Kincaid saw Flint beside the grave, and said:

'I guess you heard, Matt?'

Flint nodded, and Kincaid jerked his head at the ranch-house.

He said one word only: 'Trouble!'

Flint passed him and mounted the steps to the big house. He pushed open the door and went to the living-room, carrying his stetson in his hand. Sabina was there, but she was not alone.

Flint felt his hackles rise. Reece Berry always had that effect on him, the effect of a red rag on a bull. Swift anger surged through him, making the veins stand out like knots in his neck. They were opposites by nature, built to hate one another, and enmity was instinctive. Berry felt it too, though no tension showed in his languid pose; only his eyes showed the spark that Flint's entrance had set off.

Flint dropped his hat on the table and turned to Sabina Lomax, wondering briefly at Berry's presence there.

'I was sorry to hear about your father,' he said awkwardly. 'I guess you know you have my sympathy. He was a fine man.' He had meant to say more, but the words stuck. And that wasn't only due to Berry being in the room – Flint had never felt at ease with Lomax's daughter.

She made a faint smile for him, but it contained no warmth. Her reply was conventional and the silence dragged out. Flint had a flash of intuition; he had interrupted something between these two. Lomax had hated the sight of Berry and warned him to stay away from Sabina; now, with Lomax hardly cold, Berry was making himself at home in the house.

Sabina seemed to read his mind, for she said, calmly: 'Reece is here at my invitation.'

There was nothing Flint could say to that; she was her own boss now. He pulled out the wad of notes Lomax had given him and dropped them on the table, beside his stetson.

'No sale at Blue Rocks,' he explained. 'I got there too late.'

Berry straddled a chair, chin resting on folded arms, watching Flint intently. A half-smoked cigarette drooped from his lips. He was young, well-dressed, handsome; only his eyes belied the pose he carefully maintained. Dark, almost black eyes, sharp and alert for every movement. He carried two guns and sold them to whoever paid him highest, a professional gunman. Flint wondered: Could Sabina be in love with him?

Sabina said: 'You might as well know, Flint. I'm making changes at the Horseshoe.'

Flint gave her his attention. This was what he wanted to know, but he would have preferred that Berry didn't sit in on it. She was a beautiful woman, he thought, but it was a wild, gypsy beauty. With her dark skin and long eyelashes, she might have been mistaken for a Mexican. A headstrong girl, self-willed, too ready to break out now that parental control had been removed.

Lomax had always kept her well under his thumb; perhaps he'd been too strict, for her eyes held a gleam of excitement – she was ripe to break loose and prove she held the reins at Horseshoe. Another thing, Flint noticed: she had prettied herself up – for Berry?

Her silky hair gleamed, jet-black, off-set by one white rose. Her shoulders were smooth and bare, her dress tight and clinging; and Berry was smiling, aware of her beauty, approving.

She said: 'You're fired, Flint. I'm making Reece foreman in your place.'

She peeled off some notes from the wad he had

brought back from Blue Rocks, and held them out for him.

'A month's pay – now get off my land!'

Flint took the money, folded it carefully and thrust it deep into his shirt pocket. He could not trust himself to speak. He turned, looking at Berry, who grinned and drawled:

'I reckon you're finished with Horseshoe, Flint. How d'yuh like it?'

Flint said bluntly: 'I don't.'

He trembled with anger. This was Berry's doing. All the work he had put in on the ranch, under Lomax, stood for nothing now. His tongue had a bitter edge to it.

'Your father wouldn't figure it this way. He asked me to look out for you, Sabina.'

Her eyes clouded at the mention of her father. She knew sadness, a sense of loss – but something else too. The feeling of freedom. And that was uppermost in her mind.

'I can look out for myself,' she replied calmly. 'I'm going to show Rimrock that I can run the ranch just as well as my father.'

Berry flicked his cigarette butt into the fireplace, and added 'I'm the one that's going to take care of Sabina, Flint!' Flint picked up his stetson and ran his fingers round the brim. He was tense, and it was only by exerting all his self-control that he stopped himself from flying at Berry's throat. Sabina moved across the room and drew the

21

curtains over the window. Flint and Berry regarded one another with open antagonism. Flint appeared stolid and clumsy opposite Berry's slim and agile form; one was slow and honest, the other quick and sharp.

They stared at each other across the unpolished table. The twin oil lamps threw yellow light across their faces, making Flint's square and rugged, Berry's smooth and handsome. But their eyes revealed one quality in common, a mutual hatred.

Flint said: 'Sabina. Are you sure your father's death was an accident?'

She stared blankly.

'What do you mean, Matt?'

It was the first time she had called him by the name his friends used. He knew then that his question had shaken her, that till that moment she had not suspected there might have been foul play.

'Dad's horse stumbled and he took a fall,' Sabina said slowly. She seemed to be trying to imagine what had happened, to remember all the details. 'His head hit a rock and he was killed instantly.'

Flint asserted: 'He was too good a rider to take a fall.' Berry lit another cigarette, broke the match between his fingers and looked down at the pieces.

'You've got it all wrong, Flint,' he said deliber-

22

ately. 'You're imagining things. Sure, Lomax was a good rider, but accidents can happen to the best horsemen. I found him myself, out on the range, so I know how it was. His horse found a gopher hole and shook him clean out of the saddle, and, like Sabina said, his head struck an outcrop of rock.'

Flint looked steadily at Reece Berry. 'So, it was you who found him . . .'

'Sure it was.'

That settled it as far as Sabina was concerned. She couldn't doubt Berry's word.

'It was an accident,' she said firmly. 'Please don't refer to the incident again.'

Flint remembered the talk in town, and turned back to Sabina. 'I stopped in Rimrock on the way here. The news has got around already. Storey and Buchan were working up a mob to move in and take over Horseshoe land. I reckon you're going to have trouble with them. They figure a woman can't stop them the way Lomax did.'

Berry laughed shortly, an unpleasant sound, and touched his gun butts.

'I'll take care of trouble-makers, Flint. You needn't lose any sleep over it – remember, I'm foreman of the Horseshoe now!'

Sabina's eyes flashed.

'Ben Storey will get a shock if he tries to grab my range,' she said stormily. 'I'm keeping the Horseshoe, even if it means gunplay.'

There didn't seem to be any more to say. Flint put on his hat and moved for the door.

'I'll get my things from the bunkhouse,' he said. 'If yuh need me any time, I'll be in town, Sabina.' His eyes met Berry's, and he added stiffly: 'If any harm comes to her, you'll have me to settle with. Don't forget that.'

He closed the door behind him and stepped into the night. The bunkhouse was fifteen yards away, lighted, quieter than Flint remembered it before. He stood in the yard for some minutes, cooling off; filled his pipe and lit it. The tobacco soothed him, calmed the anger inside him, and he entered the bunkhouse with an even temper.

Men greeted him quietly.

'Glad you're back, Matt. This is a hell of a mess – any idea what's going to happen?'

They crowded round him, lean, tanned men, hardened by the life they led, normally easy-going but their faces overlaid with anxiety. Flint waited for silence, took his pipe from his mouth and said:

'I'm leaving. Reece Berry will be foreman in my place.' They didn't like that. Kincaid swore, and said:

'Then I'm leaving, too!'

Flint shook his head.

'Keep your heads. No one need leave on my account, and the Horseshoe needs all of you. Storey and Buchan will be starting trouble. You figure Lomax would want yuh to desert his daughter when she needs help most?'

Kincaid opened his mouth to speak, and closed it again. Someone said: 'I don't fancy taking orders from Berry.'

Flint, rolling his blankets, replied: 'You'll get used to it.' He threw his few possessions into a hold-all and straightened up. He felt a lump form in his throat; the Horseshoe had been his home for a long time, he'd got used to the place and had taken it for granted. He swallowed hard, wondering if he'd ever come back, and told himself it was time he moved on – a man had no right to get deeply attached to one place. Maybe it would do him good to be shaken out of his rut.

He slung the blanket-roll over his shoulder and walked to the door. Kincaid called:

'Luck, Matt.'

'Hell,' said Flint. 'I'll be seeing you in Rimrock.' He went out, shutting the broad door of the bunkhouse like a man shutting out memories. The light from the windows showed him to his roan. He strapped down the blankets and hold-all behind the saddle, mounted, and rode slowly out of the patio.

He was leaving the Horseshoe ... maybe for good. He threw that thought from him. He'd promised Lomax to look after his daughter. Along the trail, he looked back. Two shadows made a dark patch against the yellow oblong of light from the house, Sabina's and Berry's. Flint's lips made a tight, thin line. He didn't like leaving the girl alone with Reece Berry.

The stars came out, making faint pinpricks of light in the dark sky. It was a warm evening, with no wind, and the silence of the prairie had something eternal about it. Flint's thoughts reverted to Sabina. Had he failed her in some way? More than once, Lomax had hinted he wouldn't object if Flint married Sabina and took over the Horseshoe after him, but, somehow, he end Sabina had never hit it off.

It was strange, he thought, how he never felt at ease in her presence. With Nora, now, he could relax, enjoy her company without that feeling of tension he always had with Sabina. Maybe, if he'd tried harder, she wouldn't now be with Reece Berry . . . .

Well, it was no good worrying about it. Matthew Flint shrugged off his mood and rode on to Rimrock.

3

TROUBLE IN TOWN

Flint did not take up Nora's offer of work immediately, but hung around Rimrock's saloons. He took a room at the hotel and waited to see what would happen. A couple of days passed, and he became bored with doing nothing; it was a new experience for Flint to have time on his hands, and he didn't like it. At the Horseshoe, he had always been up to his ears in work.

He was tempted to ride out to the Lazy S and sign on with Dan Hurst, but he didn't want to be tied down too soon. Trouble was in the air and Sabina might need him; he had promised Lomax to stand by her, and Flint was a man who kept his promises. So he kicked his heels and waited.

It was morning again, and Flint lounged on the boardwalk, sunning himself and idly watching the scene on Main Street. Few men stopped to speak

27

to him. Rimrock was taking sides, Horseshoe against Storey and his friends, and Flint was an unknown quantity, belonging to neither one nor the other. Sheriff Arnold pointedly avoided him.

The town was quiet. A few women carried their shopping baskets from store to store. A dog scratched itself. Outside the livery stables, a hostler scrubbed down a piebald mare. A light wind stirred the dust, and, further along the boardwalk, three men shot dice.

Flint's gaze rested on a slim, girlish figure coming across the street. His rugged face, sombre from brooding, softened in a smile as he recognized Nora Hurst. She came straight up to him, and said:

'Hello, Matt. How's it feel to be a free man?'

'Not so good,' he confessed. 'I'm a man who enjoys being in harness.'

She nodded.

'Our offer still stands, Matt. There's a job waiting for you at the Lazy S.'

He hesitated, then said: 'Thanks. I'm grateful, but—' He left the rest unfinished.

Nora's brown eyes looked searchingly at him. 'Still a Horseshoe rider, Matt? Even though Sabina fired you? You can't hang around doing nothing for the rest of your life. Is it – Sabina?'

Her tone puzzled him. There was a sharpness to it he would not have expected from her.

'I promised Lomax I'd look out for his daughter

after he'd gone,' he explained slowly. 'A promise is a promise.'

'She's beautiful, of course,' Nora said. 'I expect you've noticed? Too bad she seems to have no further use for you – sort of leaves you in mid-air, doesn't it, Matt?'

'Sort of,' Flint agreed.

'Well—' Nora took a deep breath, turning away. She looked back, quickly, and added:

'Sabina's in town. I saw her buying dresses, the kind of thing to take a man's eye. I thought you'd be interested.'

Nora went on her way, leaving Flint to stare after her. He thought about Sabina; although Lomax had never kept his daughter short of anything she really needed, he had always been strict with her. Money for fine clothes had not been included in Lomax's schedule of necessities, and Sabina would not be long in making up for that omission. Flint thought there would be big changes at the Horseshoe now that a woman was in charge.

A tall man with a long jaw came striding down the street. Kincaid. And he looked angry.

'What's happened now?' Flint asked. 'Berry been getting in your hair?'

Kincaid spat, then said explosively:

'I'm fired! More than half the old Horseshoe riders are fired. Paid off and told to clear out – how d'yuh like that?' It took a little time for Flint

29

to believe it. Surely, Sabina couldn't be such a fool?

'Storey will like this,' he said. 'I can imagine him rubbing his hands and getting ready to move in on Horseshoe.' Kincaid scowled, balling his fists.

'Storey won't like it one little bit, Matt. Reece Berry is hiring new men – his sort of *hombre* – gunmen. The Horseshoe is getting ready to fight . . . .'

Flint said: 'Fighting with guns won't save the ranch. It takes work, hard work, and plenty of it. I can't see Berry's friends riding herd on cattle.'

Kincaid grunted, pointing across the street. 'Talk of the devil!'

Reece Berry and Sabina were walking down Main Street, followed by half-a-dozen rough looking men. Berry was slick as a city dude in tailored pants and black shirt and a white felt Stetson. Sabina Lomax wore a gay dress with a flower in her hair and a gleam in her eyes; her body swayed from the hips as she moved.

Kincaid said: 'The new Horseshoe outfit – Lomax must be turning in his grave.'

Flint let his gaze travel beyond Sabina, to the men Berry had hired. Each one of them looked tough; unshaven, dirty, they walked with a swagger, equipped with two guns apiece. Not one of them would have been taken on Horseshoe's payroll if Lomax still held the reins.

They halted just outside Dobie's saloon and mounted the boardwalk. The gunmen grouped themselves behind Berry and Sabina. Berry drew his Colt and loosed off a shot, firing into the air. They waited.

Gradually, a crowd formed. Men came out of stores and saloons to see what the gunshot meant. They saw Sabina, with the new Horseshoe crew, and stopped to listen. Flint saw Nora with her father; Ben Storey and Buchan side by side; Sheriff Arnold; Webb with another of the small ranchers; some of the riders Sabina had sacked. It made quite a gathering.

Kincaid looked at Flint, who nodded, and together they joined the crowd on Main Street. It was Sabina who did the talking. She said, calmly: 'I've heard talk of some of you grabbing my land, that's why I'm here. I don't want you running away with the idea that because I'm a woman, Horseshoe is finished. Remember, I'm a Lomax, too!'

She paused, sought out Ben Storey and looked him straight in the eye.

'I'm running the Horseshoe now and I'm keeping what I hold. Reece is the new foreman and he's hired a few men handy with guns – that's to show I mean business. Get this straight – make trouble for me and I fight! Anyone trying to take Horseshoe land or cattle will be met with lead.'

She placed her hands on her hips, tossed back her head, and laughed.

31

'Do I make myself clear? If you want range war . . . you can have it! I'm ready for anything. That's all I have to say. You've been warned to keep off and I'd advise you to take heed of my warning. All right, Reece, let's go.'

She started to move away, but Storey shouted:

'You, Arnold – ain't you nothing to say about that? She's threatening a shooting war. Maybe she ain't heard we've got a lawman in Rimrock?'

Sabina halted on the steps, looking at the sheriff. One of Berry's men drew his gun and pointed it idly at the crowd. Arnold hesitated, then muttered:

'I guess Miss Lomax doesn't mean any harm. She's a right to protect her own property.'

Sabina swung round on Storey.

'You see? The Horseshoe is still a force to be reckoned with in Rimrock!'

The crowd parted as Berry's gunmen came down into the street. Sabina moved for her horse, followed by Berry. Whispers ran through the silence; men shrugged uneasily; Storey and Buchan were talking in a corner and Storey beckoned over Webb to join them.

Flint was on his own, near enough in the centre of the street, and Reece Berry had to pass him to reach his horse. Their eyes met and hatred flamed nakedly. Berry jeered:

'Looks like you're a back number, Flint! Why don't yuh leave town? You're not wanted—'

Flint's fist came up and landed square in Berry's face, driving him back a pace. He said, coldly:

'You figure you can make me leave?'

Berry's right hand dropped to his gun-butt with lightning speed, but he did not draw the weapon. Another voice spoke from behind Flint:

'I've a bead on yuh, Berry!'

It was Kincaid, and he had his gun in his hand, pointed at Berry. Flint waited, angry, his hands clenched.

'If yuh want to continue this,' he said, 'it's fists, not guns.' Berry snarled and lunged forward, striking for Flint's jaw. Behind him, Sabina shouted:

'Take him, Reece – show him who's running Horseshoe now!' But neither Berry nor Flint needed encouragement. Natural enemies, they flew at each other like springs uncoiled. They had been spoiling for the fight a long time, and both were glad it had come.

Matt Flint warded of Berry's blow and slugged a couple of punches to his body. For some minutes both men, crazed with hatred, stood toe to toe and hurled bone-bruising blows at each other. A ring of men formed about them, cheering and catcalling. Then Berry realized he was getting the worst of the exchange; he backed away, panting for breath.

Flint glared at him and plunged forward, arms

swinging wildly. Berry's languid pose left him; his eyes became narrow slits, dark and hate-filled. A trickle of blood ran from his mouth and his handsome face was marked where Flint had hit him. He danced on his feet, weaving in and out, throwing hard blows to Flint's head and moving back out of reach.

Flint grunted, his eyes misting redly. Berry was the faster of the two men, and intended to keep him at a distance. He moved steadily forward, closing the gap. Berry was young and strong, very quick, but Flint had more weight behind his punches – he needed to get to grips and finish the fight.

Kincaid's voice sounded over the shouting of the crowd: 'Any *hombre* horning in on this fight had better think twice – I've a gun in my hand that says they're going to slug it out on their own.'

Berry was slinging fast, desperate punches to Flint's head, trying to hold him off. And Sabina was shouting:

'Kill him, Reece – kill him!'

Flint got a hold on Berry's shirt and dragged him into range, smashing his other fist into the handsome face. Berry slugged Flint twice, low down, and kicked savagely at his ankles. Flint, weakened, toppled sideways – and Berry leapt through the air, climbing on top of him as both men fell to the ground.

Flint landed on his back, grasped Berry's shoulders and threw him over his head. He came up on one knee, covered with dust and gasping for air. Berry kicked out wildly. Flint caught at the ankle and twisted; Berry cried out in pain and writhed away.

They both stood up, spitting out dust and glaring. Then Flint moved in for the kill. He put all his weight behind his fists, driving heavy blows into Berry's face, forcing him back against the ring of onlookers. Berry sagged, near exhaustion, and Flint swung a right that took the gunman under the jaw with a loud crack. Berry dropped like a sack of potatoes and did not stir.

Flint stepped back, lowering his hands; he turned away as someone laughed. Then a voice snapped: 'Matt – look out!'

He turned to see Sabina lunging for him, a crazed expression on her face and a stiletto in her hand. She was screaming:

'His face – his face! You've spoiled his face!'

Flint had no chance to protect himself. Sabina was on him before he could raise a hand, and there was little doubt she would have stabbed him if Nora Hurst had not acted. Slim, pretty Nora was no weakling. She leapt forward and seized Sabina's wrist, turning her body so that the blade passed harmlessly over Flint's shoulder. She exerted pressure till Sabina was forced to drop the knife.

Nora pushed her back and stood between her

and Flint. She said: 'That's enough, Sabina.'

Flint picked up the stiletto. It had a blade as thin as a needle and long enough to penetrate to a man's heart; the handle was silver, inlaid with mother-of-pearl. It was a beautiful, deadly weapon – like Sabina herself. He put the blade under his heel and snapped it, tossed both pieces from him.

'Thanks, Nora,' he said quietly.

Sabina Lomax trembled with a wild passion. Her face was contorted with rage and she was near to sobbing. Her shoulders heaved spasmodically and she spoke in a choked voice.

'I'll get you, Matt Flint! I'll get you for this!' Then she turned and ran to Berry, cradled his head in her arms and said, softly:

'Reece, Reece darling, I love you. We'll pay them out for what they've done to you.'

Flint stood still, his face revealing amazement. Kincaid and some of the other riders fired from the Horseshoe were eyeing Berry's new gun crew as if they'd like to mix it, too.

Sheriff Arnold pushed to the fore. Backed up by Flint and Kincaid, he was able to exert his authority.

'All right now,' he said briskly. 'The fight's over and I don't want any gunplay. Break it up. Vamoose.'

Berry was conscious again and on his feet. Sabina helped him to mount his horse. She looked back once, and cried:

36

'You'll pay for this, all of you. You'll find out that Horseshoe is still the power in Rimrock!'

They rode out of town, Sabina and Reece Berry, and the six hired gunfighters. But the manner of their riding left no doubt that they would be back.

The crowd dispersed silently. Flint sat on the boardwalk with his feet in the dusty road and someone brought him a tumbler of whisky and a wet towel. He tossed back the liquor at one gulp and wiped his face.

Ben Storey, with Buchan and Webb, came across the street. Storey said, smiling: 'Well, I guess you're in with us from now on, Flint. Horseshoe hasn't any more use for yuh.'

He grinned, his sallow face gloating. Storey had never liked Flint, because he was Lomax's foreman; but he respected his fighting ability and wanted him on his side.

Flint looked beyond the small, dark shape of Ben Storey, to Kincaid and the other riders who had worked for Lomax. He knew they were watching him, waiting for him to speak. If he threw in with Storey, they would, too. Abruptly, Flint stood up, still holding the wet towel in his hands.

He said: 'I'm not fighting Horseshoe, Ben. You're wasting your time.'

He turned and started to walk back to the hotel. Dan Hurst followed after him, calling, 'Matt, wait for me.'

Flint stopped. Hurst came abreast of him and

spoke seriously. 'You know your own mind best, Matt, but that was a fool thing to do, turning Storey down that way. You're on your own, between Horseshoe and Storey's gang, a marked man. Don't you want any friends?'

'I'll manage,' Flint said briefly.

Hurst looked worried, and ran one hand through his grey hair.

'I need a good man to help at the Lazy S. And Nora—'

'Try Kincaid,' Flint replied, and walked away.

4
MURDER!

'Damn cattle have drifted during the night,' grunted Bill Yates, staring across the plain that reached all the way from the banks of the river to the distant line of mountains.

It was a little after dawn, and Yates, with Luke Parrish, both Double U riders, were on early morning patrol.

'They won't have gone far,' Parrish drawled, making himself a cigarette one-handed. 'Steers ain't so dumb – they know there's better grazing further up.'

'Yeah, on Horseshoe land,' Yates scowled. 'Best round 'em up before there's trouble.'

'Likely, the boss won't mind an excuse to start something,' Parrish said lazily. 'Me neither. It always riled me the way Lomax had his own way in these parts.'

He was a lean, rangy man, younger than Yates.

'Buchan pays me to herd cattle, not sling lead with professionals,' Bill Yates grunted. 'I don't fancy meeting Berry on Horseshoe land.'

Parrish grinned.

'Berry won't be showing his face yet awhile, not after the marking Flint gave it. Quit worrying, Bill, we ain't going to run into Reece Berry this morning.'

They rode on, passing the boundary markers and entering Horseshoe territory. Further on, beyond a clump of pines and a low, rolling range of grassy dunes, the river bent in an oxbow. It was here, where the banks sloped down to a narrow neck of land and the grass was thick and juicy, that the missing cattle grazed.

Yates and Parrish sent their horses down the slope, getting behind the steers. Working together, swinging their stetsons and shouting, they got the cattle moving again, heading them back for the Double U range. It was slow work, with the steers reluctant to leave the oxbow.

They finally succeeded in getting them up the bank, and started the slow journey homeward. It was fully light now, with the sun still rising and no cloud in the sky. On the horizon, a heat haze blurred the peaks of the mountains.

Yates and Parrish rode leisurely behind the cattle, sometimes beating the rump of a steer with their dusty hats, sometimes spurring their mounts to chase a straggler. They were almost to the boundary markers when trouble came.

Six riders came up fast behind them, the drumming of hoofs beating an urgent tattoo through the ground. Yates swung round, grunting: 'Horseshoe!'

Parrish checked his horse, turning to face the newcomers. He let his right hand slide down to the butt of his Colt and there was a gleam in his eyes.

'Three to one,' he drawled. 'Looks like our unlucky day.'

The Horseshoe men came to a halt, ten yards away, forming half circle about them.

Yates said, softly: 'Hold yourself in, Luke. We've done nothing wrong and we don't want trouble.'

Bill Yates was forty, a careful man, and didn't like the look of the new Horseshoe outfit. He kept his hands clear of his guns as he called:

'You fellers want something?'

Their leader said: 'Yeah, those cattle! You've a hell of a nerve, trying to rustle steers right under our noses.'

He was big and broad and sat a heavy stallion, an ugly man whose face had been mauled by a bear, and his deformity was matched by his character. He wore two large-bore Colts at his waist.

Parrish flared up: 'Rustling, nothing! These are Double U steers – they drifted, and we're taking them back.'

The big man laughed, appealing to his cronies.

'You hear that, boys? They reckon on driving the cattle over to Buchan's range . . . seems to me we can't allow that!'

One of the hired gunmen started forming a noose in his lariat. 'String 'em up, Cal. String 'em up – that's the way to deal with rustlers.'

Yates sat stiffly in the saddle, taut, his hands sweating. 'Take a look at the brand,' he invited. 'Our Double U's plain enough to see.'

Calhoun, the big man, made no attempt to look at the cattle. 'Brands ain't of any consequence,' he said deliberately. 'Our orders are, any cattle found on Horseshoe range belong to Miss Lomax. That makes you rustlers!'

'Like hell it does,' Parrish snorted. 'Wait till Buchan hears about this.'

Yates was uneasy. He was no longer young, and Parrish was hot-tempered; these men were just looking for an excuse to start something. They were edging nearer, taking their time over it, because they were six to two. They could afford to play cat-and-mouse. Suddenly, all Yates wanted was to turn his horse and run for it.

Calhoun said, grinning, so that his ugly face seemed even more diabolical than ordinarily: 'Buchan won't be hearing it from you two!'

Parrish went for his gun, but he wasn't fast enough. Calhoun had a heavy Colt in his hand before Parrish got his clear of its holster. He fired once, and the shell smashed into Parrish's chest.

His horse reared, throwing him, and bolted riderless.

Bill Yates wheeled his horse, spurring it madly. He loosed off wild shots as he rode at breakneck speed for safety. Shells whined after him, but he escaped unscathed. A bitter rage swept through him; Luke Parrish's death had been cold-blooded murder – and someone was going to pay for that!

Calhoun called back his men as they started after Yates. 'Let him go,' said the ugly man. 'Reece wants the story to get to Buchan. The Lomax gal is taking the blame for this!' One of the men dismounted and turned over Parrish's body with his boot.

'Dead,' he pronounced carelessly. 'A nice shot, Cal.'

Calhoun looked pleased as he pushed a fresh shell into the empty chamber of his gun and holstered it.

'I don't often miss,' he grunted. 'All right, leave the body where it is – the buzzards will take care of it soon enough. We'll get back and report to Reece.'

They turned back for the ranch.

'A smart *hombre*, Reece,' he said, thinking aloud. 'He makes trouble for the Horseshoe and the Lomax gal gets blamed. Then he takes over the ranch himself. Oh, yes, a real clever *hombre* is Reece Berry!'

He rode on, thinking of the bonus that Berry had promised him for this morning's work. Meanwhile, Bill Yates had reached the Double U and was telling the story to Buchan. Buchan's surly face was livid.

'Steal my cattle! Kill my riders! By thunder, she'll pay for this. Saddle up, boys, we're going for the sheriff.'

But he broke the journey to Rimrock to call on Ben Storey and get his backing; and Storey's eyes gleamed, for he thought he saw the beginning of the end for Horseshoe.

Matthew Flint was alone at the bar of Dobie's saloon when the sound of riders echoed on Main Street. He left his glass on the counter and crossed to the window to see who had come to town in suck a hurry. Outside, a flurry of dust obscured his view. He pushed through the batwings, on to the board-walk, and stood a moment, letting his eyes take in the scene.

The dust was settling again. Half-a-dozen horses milled around in front of the sheriff's office; he recognized the riders – Buchan's men. Three men hurried into the law office, calling for Arnold. Buchan, Ben Storey, and a middle-aged man with anger in his face. Flint knew him casually, one of the Double U outfit, a man named Yates.

Flint started for the sheriff's office as men

44

came running up to form a crowd on the street. Noisy questions were asked.

'What's happened? What's going on?'

'Looks like trouble to me – likely the Horseshoe again!'

One of the Double U riders called out: 'Luke Parrish was murdered by Horseshoe. We're getting the sheriff to bring in his killer.'

Flint thought: So it's happened already, and quickened his pace. He pushed through to the front of the crowd. From the law office came the sound of heated voices; Buchan's loud and surly, Yates' angry. Arnold sounded flustered. And, in the background, Ben Storey was slyly urging Buchan to violence.

Flint went up the steps and into the office. Storey turned and glared at him.

'What d'you want here, Flint?' he demanded.

'Just seeing yuh don't make any mistakes, Ben. You're liable to think of yourself first and justice second.'

Arnold seemed glad of Flint's support, and looked gratefully at him.

Buchan said: 'You getting up a posse, Arnold? My man was shot down in cold blood, and I want a hanging. I can do it without yuh, but I'd prefer to have the law with me. And I'm in no mood to waste time.'

Arnold replied, mildly: 'A little while back you said you had no use for me. You've changed your tune awful sudden.' Buchan snorted angrily.

'There's been a man killed. You're sheriff, and it's your duty—'

Arnold snapped: 'Yuh don't have to tell me my duty, Buchan. I'll ride out to Horseshoe with you.' He went to the door and called: 'Ted, saddle my horse, pronto.' Then, turning back to Buchan, said: 'Shut up! You, Yates, tell me exactly what happened.'

Flint and Arnold listened while Bill Yates told of the drifting cattle and Calhoun's action. Storey interjected quickly:

'On the Lomax girl's orders, mark you! Don't overlook that, Sheriff.'

Flint thought the position looked bad for Sabina. He fumbled for his pipe, filled the bowl clumsily and lit up.

Arnold said, grimly: 'I'm overlooking nothing, Ben. Now, you *hombres* get out of here – I want to talk to Flint alone.'

'Flint!' exploded Buchan. 'What's he got to do with it?'

'Outside,' the sheriff repeated.

Bill Yates went out, followed by the small figure of Ben Storey. Buchan's large bulk filled the doorway; he shouted:

'I'll give you five minutes, then I'm riding for a showdown.' Arnold kicked the door shut.

Flint dropped into a chair, sucking on his pipe and watching the sheriff. He couldn't guess what was coming.

Arnold said, suddenly: 'What do you make of this, Matt? You know Sabina better than anyone. D'you think she'll stand by a killer?'

Flint felt sorry for Arnold. He wasn't man enough for the sheriff's job; he was too old to buck ruthless men.

'Sabina's wild,' Flint said carefully, 'but I don't reckon she's bad. My guess is that Berry is behind this. Remember, you've only heard one side of the story so far.'

Arnold nodded, relieved. He waited a moment, then said 'I don't reckon I cut much of a figure in Rimrock, Matt. I'm in the wrong job, but that doesn't mean I'm yellow. I'm going through with this, and I'll do my duty. What I want to know is, will you take on the job of deputy? I'd feel a lot happier with you backing my play.'

Flint was surprised by the offer, after the way Arnold had been ignoring him the past few days. He smoked his pipe and looked at the sheriff – a small, bony man with thinning hair and skin like parchment. He could, he realized, take over the law office if he wanted.

Arnold said, 'You've left Horseshoe now, Matt, and you've turned down Storey's offer. That leaves you placed between them, right in line for any trouble that's coming. It would strengthen your position to wear a law badge.'

Flint nodded in agreement; it would at that. He

considered the idea briefly, and rejected it. He
wanted to help Sabina – he couldn't afford to have
his hands tied. The time might come when, as
deputy sheriff, it would be his duty to move
against Sabina Lomax. He couldn't take the risk.

Arnold went on: 'As I see it, big trouble is liable
to come any moment. Range war, feuding, innocent people dying. That's what I want to stop.'

Flint rose to his feet.

'Sorry, Sheriff,' he said quietly, 'I can't take the
job. I'll ride with yuh to Horseshoe and back you
up, but not as deputy. We've the same interest in
common – to stop wholesale massacre on the
ranges – and you can rely on me to do anything I
can to that end. But I must be free to act in my
own way.'

Arnold didn't try to hide his disappointment.

'A pity, Matt,' he said with a sigh; and, suddenly,
he seemed an old man.

Flint put his hand on Arnold's shoulder.

'You've nothing to be ashamed of; a man can
only do his best. I reckon Rimrock is lucky in
having you in this office.'

The sheriff said, gruffly: 'Let's ride, Matt.'

He opened the door and both men went down
the steps to the street. Ted was holding the reins
of Arnold's horse; the sheriff climbed into the
saddle as Flint took long strides to the stables to
get his own mount.

Buchan said, irritably: 'Well, what are we waiting for now?'

Arnold gave him a straight look. 'Matt Flint,' he answered. Buchan looked sideways at Ben Storey, who said, meanly: 'I figure we don't need Flint on this trip.'

Arnold's voice held a note of authority as he replied: 'Well, he's coming anyway.'

Just then, Flint rode up on his bay roan. Arnold turned to look over the crowd, counting the riders ready saddled.

'Me and Flint,' he said. 'Yates and Buchan. That's all – the rest of you cool your heels.'

Buchan glared at the sheriff.

'My boys are riding along,' he stormed. 'It's one of my riders that was murdered.'

Arnold said: 'This is a posse, not a lynching mob. Your riders can head back for the Double U, Buchan. I'm not arguing, I'm telling you!'

Buchan was furious. He'd brought in the law, and now he had to obey. He gave his men new orders.

Storey grunted: 'I'm riding with yuh, Arnold, so don't try to stop me.'

The sheriff looked at Storey, then at Flint. He smiled faintly. 'All right, Ben – I guess Buchan needs someone to hold his hand.'

They set off, Buchan and Ben Storey together, Bill Yates riding between Flint and Arnold. The posse made a fast pace, leaving the winding river and using the direct trail to Horseshoe. Miles passed, miles of open grassland, dotted here and there with pine and cottonwood. The sun was high and the air hot and stifling.

Flint thought ahead to the meeting with Sabina, and didn't like it a bit. There was trouble in the air. Arnold would try to handle it carefully, he knew. Buchan, separated from his riders, wouldn't be shouting so loud; there was a long streak of yellow in him. Storey was too cunning to reveal his hand openly. It was in Bill Yates that the danger lay; Yates had seen his friend shot down and was all set for a showdown.

Flint decided it was Yates he had to watch.

5
THE NEXT MOVE

'I reckon we'll stop to pick up Luke Parrish's body,' Arnold said abruptly.

He was looking away to the left, where buzzards hovered in the sky.

Yates swore. 'The swine! They couldn't even bury him -just left him for the buzzards to pick to pieces.'

The posse, led by Arnold and Flint, wheeled left, riding down the bank between pine trees towards the silver river. Parrish lay where he had fallen, gun-arm under him and his Colt jerked loose from its holster. The dead man's horse had returned and was grazing nearby; it was the horse that had kept the carrion birds aloft for the past hours.

Sheriff Arnold inspected the body critically. 'Went for his gun,' he remarked. 'Shot from the front, through the chest. Guess he just wasn't fast enough.'

Yates said, angrily: 'They didn't give him a chance – it was murder.'

Flint roped Parrish's horse and removed the saddle. He lifted the dead man on to the animal's back and secured him fast.

Storey looked round. 'Rider's coming,' he said.

The posse straightened up, waiting. There was tension in them. Flint manoeuvred his roan to be near Yates, looping the free end of the rope from Parrish's horse to his saddle horn.

Arnold looked round at Buchan and Storey, and said: 'I don't want you fellers starting gunplay. I'll do the talking.' Flint was watching the riders. Sabina was in the lead, next to an ugly man on a stallion horse.

Yates spat: 'Calhoun!'

Flint studied the killer and was shocked that Sabina should ride openly with such a man, not on account of his disfigured face, but because his badness was plain to see. He was no more than a brute with the lust to kill.

Sabina Lomax reined in her mount, facing the sheriff. She wore a white shirt with a smart riding skirt and a sombrero. She was beautiful to look at, but her beauty was marred by a hardness in her face. Flint could read no sign of compromise in her expression.

Arnold said: 'This is a bad business, Miss Lomax.' Calhoun laughed harshly.

'Don't let 'em scare yuh,' he said to the girl.

'They've got nothing on me. Ain't that right, boys?' He appealed to the five gunmen grouped behind him.

Flint's lips tightened. If this meeting developed into a gunfight, the posse was liable to get the worst of it. These men were too ready to start throwing lead. He kept a sharp watch on Bill Yates.

Arnold gestured at Parrish's body. 'A man's been murdered—'

Again, Calhoun laughed. He was a large man, deep-chested, and the sound was like the rumbling of a volcano.

'Murder's a big word, Sheriff. Parrish went for his gun after I caught him rustling—'

'I'll do the talking,' Sabina Lomax interrupted shortly. She wouldn't look at Flint, but directed her remarks at Arnold. Reece Berry was not present.

'Buchan and Storey and some of the other ranchers were threatening to take my land,' Sabina said. 'You heard them yourself, Sheriff. And you heard me warn them that I'd fight back. Well, an eye for an eye is the law of the west, and I gave orders that any cattle drifting on to my range automatically become my cattle. Calhoun was obeying my orders when he stopped Parrish driving the steers back.'

She paused, taking breath.

'Parrish went for his gun first. Calhoun beat him

to the draw, and that's all there is to it. We have witnesses that Parrish started the gunplay—'

'That so?' said Arnold, leaning forward.

There was a growl of assent from the five men backing Calhoun.

Arnold twisted in his saddle, looking at Yates. 'What d'yuh have to say to that?' he asked.

Bill Yates couldn't take his eyes off Calhoun, and there was the glint of hatred in them.

'Sure Luke went for his gun; wouldn't you, against a professional? It was murder, right enough. Calhoun forced the play on him.'

Calhoun sneered: 'How would you know, feller? You were high-tailing it too fast to see the action!'

Yates' face went white. 'Why, you—'

And his right hand dropped for his gun. Flint acted promptly, dropping his own hand over Yates' and smothering the draw.

'Keep your temper, Bill,' he said easily. 'These *hombres* only want the chance to start something.'

Buchan rode forward, bringing his horse level with Arnold's. 'You see, Sheriff? Calhoun's a killer. He'd have dropped Yates as he did Parrish. I demand that you bring him in.' Arnold looked troubled. Bringing in Calhoun was easier said that done. He looked quickly at Flint, then said: 'Calhoun, I want—'

Sabina Lomax interrupted him.

'Save it, Sheriff. Calhoun was acting under

54

orders, protecting my rights. The Horseshoe sticks together, as you'll find out. Try to take Calhoun and you'll have a shooting war on your hands!'

She untied a leather bag from her saddle horn and tossed it to Buchan.

'Two hundred dollars in gold,' she said calmly. 'That should cover any inconvenience you may have had. Now get off my land and stay off.'

There was a hush that lasted fully thirty seconds, then Buchan roared:

'Damn you, Sabina! If you figure you can buy off murder as easy as that, you're making a mistake!' He swore luridly. 'The Double U will settle in lead!'

Calhoun's ugly face twisted in the semblance of a smile. 'Big talk, *hombre*. Let's see yuh put the actions to it.' And he waited, gun-hand clawing the air above his heavy Colt. Buchan cooled off fast.

'This is your fault, Arnold,' he accused. 'If I'd brought my outfit along, as I wanted, Calhoun would be swinging from a tree by now.'

Ben Storey inserted a word, judging the moment right to make more trouble.

'There's the cattle, Sheriff. You letting Horseshoe keep Buchan's cattle?'

Sabina rounded on him quickly.

'They ran off when the shooting started. Likely they're back on Double U ground now.'

Sheriff Arnold moved restlessly in the saddle.

55

Damn it, he thought, I can't manhandle a woman! She's no right to act this way. Now, if it were a man talking . . . .

He was at a complete loss, not knowing how to handle the situation. Sabina had the edge on him – and she knew it.

Abruptly, Arnold wheeled his horse about, and said, briefly: 'Back to town.'

The Horseshoe crowd watched them ride off. Storey and Buchan ignored the sheriff and angled away towards the Double U.

Flint turned over Parrish's body to Bill Yates.

He said: 'Reckon you'd like the burying of him, Bill.'

Yates nodded, silently. There was anger working up in him, against Horseshoe – and especially against Sabina Lomax for backing Calhoun.

Flint said: 'I reckon she'll come to her senses in time. Let it wait, Bill. This is Berry's work, not Sabina's. She'll break with him, one day – and Calhoun will keep till then.'

Yates didn't answer. He took the reins of Parrish's horse and rode after Buchan. Flint sighed heavily.

Sheriff Arnold said: 'What else could I do, Matt? I don't want range war in Rimrock.'

'She called the tune, all right,' Flint grunted. 'I only wish I could see the end of this business.'

He didn't speak after that, but his thoughts were busy. Sabina had scored off the law, and that

56

wasn't going to do anyone any good. He was uneasy for her. Reece Berry seemed to have her right under his thumb – and Berry was crooked. He wondered what the next move would be.

Sabina Lomax arrived back at the Horseshoe ranch in a troubled state of mind. To be sure, she was pleased with her triumph over the sheriff, but her pleasure was tempered by the knowledge that a man had died. And she had the normal amount of respect for the law; it worried her a little that she should be forced into a position where she had to stand against the sheriff.

Calhoun and the others had left her shortly after the posse rode away, and she continued back to the ranch alone. She dismounted and turned her horse into the corral. She didn't like Calhoun; there was something about him that frightened her – in fact, if Berry had not insisted, she would never have put the ugly man on her payroll.

Crossing the patio, to the house, she paused a moment by the lone pine. She wondered, uneasily, what her father would have thought of the present situation. He had ruled Rimrock with the iron fist in a velvet glove; he had never resorted to killing. Sabina turned away from the grave of Piers Lomax and hurried into the house. Reece understood these things – he would comfort her.

Reece Berry sat alone in the big living room with the puma-skin rugs and plain, timbered furniture. He was playing patience with a pack of well-thumbed cards and smoking a cigarette. By his side, on the table, stood a tumbler and a half-empty bottle of whisky; cigarette butts littered the floor.

He looked up, said casually, 'Hello, darling,' and went on with his game.

Sabina removed her hat, allowing dark hair to fall about her shoulders. Smiling, she went to Berry and kissed him lightly. He pushed her away.

'Not now, Sabina – my face still hurts.'

One eye was dark and swollen, his lip cut and sore; there were bruises on both cheeks and his nose looked as if it would never recover its normal shape. Altogether, Flint had spoiled Berry's handsome features.

'My poor Reece,' Sabina said softly. 'When 1 think of what Matt Flint did—'

At the mention of Flint's name, Berry scowled and pushed back his chair. He spilled his cards across the table.

'I'll settle with Flint,' he said harshly. 'Next time we meet, it'll be guns, not fists!'

The venom in his voice disturbed Sabina; since he had moved into the ranch-house, she was learning that Reece Berry had a quite different nature from the polished, languid pose he assumed. Inwardly, she felt glad he had not ridden to meet the posse. Berry crushed out his cigarette, looked at her, and demanded:

'Well, what happened?'

'It happened just as you said it would, Reece. Sheriff Arnold wanted to arrest Calhoun. When I told him the Horseshoe would stand by Calhoun, he backed down.'

Berry laughed.

'It's no more than I expected. Arnold took orders from your father, and he'll take orders from you. Horseshoe is still the power in Rimrock – and it's going to stay that way.'

Sabina said; 'Calhoun. Do we really need him, Reece? He scares me.'

Berry watched her face, reading her mind. Suddenly, he smiled. 'Cal's all right, darling. You mustn't judge him by his looks. He takes my orders without question, that's the important thing. I'll see he doesn't bother you.'

Sabina worried the point.

'He killed a man.'

'Parrish – a Buchan rider! Are you forgetting Buchan is your enemy, that he and Storey are out to grab Horseshoe? Calhoun did you a favour when he shot Parrish. It'll show them we mean business.'

Sabina sighed unhappily. 'I suppose you're right.'

'Of course I am,' Berry said sharply. 'Sabina – you trust me don't you? I'm only doing what's best, I want to make Horseshoe safe for you. You do understand that?'

She went swiftly to his side.

'Reece, I love you so . . . be kind to me.'

He put his arm about her and caressed her, and she kissed him passionately.

'You're all I have now,' Sabina said, 'with Dad gone and—'

She laid her head against his chest, trembling, and holding him. 'Reece – you do love me, don't you?'

He bent to kiss her.

'You know I do, darling—' he pushed her off 'now we have to settle the next move. You won't be safe until we have Rimrock under our thumb. Storey and Buchan won't be stopped easily, and we're not giving up without a fight. Fortunately, I have a plan. Listen . . .'

Reece Berry watched the girl closely. He was not sure how she would take his suggestion, and it was important that she agree to do just what he wanted. He smiled, regaining some of his old charm.

'This is what we'll do,' he said.

Sabina Lomax listened in silence. She did not speak, even when he had finished. Berry waited for her answer, tense, lighting a cigarette.

'It's the only thing to do, Sabina. You see that, don't you?' Still she hesitated.

'It doesn't seem—'

Berry said: 'Nothing else will stop Ben Storey now. He's out to grab Horseshoe from you. It's

60

fight, or surrender. Trust me, darling – I know what's best. After this, we'll be together, always.'

Sabina nodded. 'All right, Reece – I'll do it . . . for you!'

6

WATER

Flint, Dan Hurst and Kincaid were talking in front of Dobie's saloon on Main Street, waiting for Nora to finish her shopping expedition. The Lazy S wagon was loaded ready for the return trip to the ranch.

Hurst was saying: 'I intend to stay out of this fight, Matt. The Lazy S is a small outfit – I can't afford to be crushed between Horseshoe and Ben Storey.'

Kincaid, now Hurst's foreman, commented: 'It's the right attitude, Mr Hurst, but I'm not sure it's possible. Storey means business; he's trying to get all the small ranches to stand together – you ain't going to be popular with him. And Sabina has shown she means to hold what she's got.'

Dan Hurst snorted.

'I don't take orders from Ben!'

Flint knocked out his pipe and rubbed the bowl

shiny on his pants.

'The outlook isn't good,' he said sombrely. 'Parrish was a decent sort, and his murder sure riled the Double U men – they're not going to be satisfied till Calhoun swings. Then there's the old Horseshoe outfit. One or two have joined Storey or Buchan, some have drifted, the rest are just kicking their heels in town, waiting for the balloon to go up. They reckon they've good cause for complaint over Sabina's treatment and—'

He broke off as Nora Hurst came hurrying along the boardwalk towards them. She looked excited, even worried about something.

'Dad, Sabina and Berry are in town, and Sabina has just put up a notice outside the sheriff's office. She must be crazy – what she's doing isn't possible. It'll start a riot or—'

'Suppose,' interrupted Dan Hurst, 'that you tell us what the notice says?'

Nora checked herself, then said quietly:

'She intends to make a charge for all ranches using the river to water their cattle. She claims that because the river comes through Horseshoe land, she has a right to be paid. She's demanding fifty dollars a month from all ranches.'

Hurst and Kincaid exchanged glances. Flint rubbed his jaw thoughtfully.

'And what happens,' he asked, 'if you don't pay?'

Hurst looked relieved.

'Bluff,' he said. 'She can't do a thing about it.

The river's there, always has been and always will be. This is strong-arm stuff; if we stand together, she can't enforce it.'

Flint commented drily: 'You were saying, Dan, that you weren't going to throw in with Storey!'

Up the street, a crowd of men formed outside the sheriff's office. Angry voices were raised in protest.

Kincaid shuffled his feet.

'Maybe we'd better see what this is about,' he said. 'I'm going to take a look at that notice for myself.'

He strode off followed by Dan Hurst. Nora caught at Flint's arm and held him back.

'Keep out of this, Matt,' she pleaded. 'Berry's looking for you and he means to force a gunfight. I don't want you hurt.' Flint gazed down at her, surprised by the tense expression on her face. She looked strangely small and subdued, yet somehow determined; there was a light in her eyes he had not seen before.

'I never guessed you cared that much,' he said slowly. 'It's nice to know, Nora . . . but you can stop worrying 'cause I don't aim to get myself killed just yet.'

They moved along the boardwalk together, keeping on the far side of the street from the crowd. Flint watched Nora from the corner of his eye. She was pretty, he thought, and there was something in her that stirred him, something more than her slim feminine figure and chestnut curls, or the determined set of her chin. It was the way she seemed to fit into his life, like a second half he had never missed till that moment.

'I reckon I've been mighty slow in not seeing how you felt,' he said. 'But you see how I'm fixed just now—'

She smiled faintly.

'I'll wait, Matt. It's not for me to speak first, but I had to let you know. I couldn't bear it if anything happened to you.' He nodded, laying his hand on her arm.

'This business will finish one way or the other shortly, Nora. Then I'll be calling on yuh to speak my piece.'

Across the street, Sheriff Arnold was trying to quieten the crowd. Flint saw Reece Berry and Sabina, side by side. Dan Hurst and Kincaid had pushed to the front and were reading the notice Sabina had put up with her own hand.

Hurst, slim and grey-haired, turned to Sabina and said:

'Fifty dollars a month for taking water from the river, Miss Lomax? I reckon you must be crazy if you think you can enforce that.'

'I can!' Sabina Lomax snapped. 'This is my way of proving that Horseshoe is still the power in Rimrock. Every ranch will pay toll to me . . . or go without water!'

Hurst stared at her.

'You've got Berry's hired thugs working for you,' he said bluntly, 'but do you reckon we'll not get together and fight? You can't stop the river flowing. It'll just mean gunplay – and the sheriff fetching help from the county town.'

'You fool!' Sabina tossed back her head in a way that set her ear-rings dancing and her jet black hair flowing in wild waves. Her dark eyes gleamed. 'That's where you're wrong, Dan Hurst – I can stop the river!'

Kincaid drawled: 'Meaning just what, Sabina?'

'Meanin' Rimrock Creek,' she flashed back.

There was a sudden hush. Every man in the crowd let his thoughts dwell on the words – Rimrock Creek – and anxiety began to show in many faces as the hidden threat of that phrase struck home.

Sabina Lomax spoke again.

'I see that you know what I mean. Where the river comes down from the mountains, on to Horseshoe land, it flows through a narrow gorge called Rimrock Creek. The water only reaches your ranges after it leaves Horseshoe. Well, if you don't agree to pay me fifty dollars a month, I'll dynamite the gorge!'

She stopped, smiling, sure of herself and her power. Reece had been right; this was the way to stop Storey and Buchan. She was going to show them who was boss!

'First,' she said calmly, 'I'll blast a new path for

66

the river to take, across Horseshoe and away to the desert. Then I'll block Rimrock Creek. You'll have no water, your grass will wither and your cattle die.'

Reece Berry came forward, cigarette dangling from his mouth, eyes narrowed and hands on gunbutts.

'You've got till sundown to make up your minds,' he said harshly. 'Get together and collect the money, one man to ride out to Horseshoe with it. Fifty dollars from each ranch. If I don't get the first instalment tonight, we start blasting at dawn!'

He took Sabina's arm and walked her down the street, most of the crowd following. She took no notice of the angry words shouted at her. Outside the general store, Sabina's buck-board was parked. She waited by the horses while Berry went into the store; the town quietened, puzzled by this action. But they were not puzzled for long. Reece Berry came from the store carrying a small wooden crate containing sticks of dynamite, and a coiled length of fuse-cord.

In complete silence, he put the crate in the back of the wagon, climbed up beside Sabina, and took hold of the reins.

'Till sundown, tonight,' he said casually, and drove off. Sheriff Arnold had quite a time stopping a riot. A few men went for their horses, to ride to the outlying ranches and spread the news. Ben

Storey was suddenly to the fore, calling for a public meeting to decide on a course of action. The saloons did a brisk trade from punchers and townsfolk who decided that strong liquor was called for.

Hurst and Kincaid rejoined Flint.

'This is damnable,' the rancher exclaimed. 'You know me, Matt – I don't want trouble. But this means my livelihood. I've got to throw in with Ben now.'

Nora said, anxiously: 'But, surely, the sheriff—'

'Arnold isn't big enough to stop this,' Kincaid interrupted. 'Looks like big-scale war to me.' He added bitterly: 'Damn that hound, Berry!'

Flint nodded. 'Yeah, it's Berry who is behind this. He's sure leading Sabina by the nose.'

Hurst and Nora went off. Kincaid looked at Flint and shifted uneasily.

'I never reckoned Sabina could act this way,' he said uncomfortably. 'I always thought she was a decent sort of girl, a bit wild, but not bad at heart. I just don't understand what's got into her.'

Flint studied the tall man; his face looked longer than ever, like a man with a secret sorrow weighing him down. He guessed that Kincaid had a soft spot for Sabina.

'Reckon she'll get over it,' he said easily. 'She's upset at her father's death, and thinks she's in love with Berry. I guess she's just doing what he tells her. She'll come to her senses before long.'

68

Kincaid nodded.

'Sure hope you're right, Matt.' He paused. 'You figuring on taking sides?'

Flint said: 'I want to stop a range war, that's all I'm interested in. Besides keeping my promise to Lomax, to look out for his daughter.'

Kincaid rolled himself a cigarette.

'Let me know if there's anything I can do. You'll find me at the Lazy S.'

He walked away, after Dan Hurst. Flint went back to the hotel for lunch, and waited for Storey to hold his meeting.

It started at three o'clock. The afternoon was hot and the hall crowded. Ben Storey, black-suited and sallow-faced, stood behind a table on the platform, flanked on either side by Buchan and Webb. Inigo Webb was a small rancher, a man with sandy hair and indeterminate chin, content to follow the lead of the majority.

Storey said: 'I won't waste your time with words. You all know what we're here for, so I'll get down to business. I take it none of yuh are considering paying fifty dollars for the privilege of watering your herd?'

A growl of assent greeted this. Ben Storey smiled expansively, looking round the hall. His gaze rested on Dan Hurst.

'You, Dan,' he said. 'You're with us in this matter?' Hurst was to one side of the hall, next to Arnold.

He answered: 'I can't afford to pay. None of us can.'

Storey nodded, pleased. 'Quite so, Dan.'

But Hurst wasn't finished. He didn't like the idea of Storey running the show. He appealed to Arnold.

'Sheriff, I call on you to tell us how the law stands in this affair. Legally, can Sabina Lomax do what she threatens?'

Arnold spoke up. 'You people have my sympathy – I want yuh to know that. But, legally, my hands are tied. Miss Lomax owns the territory of which Rimrock Creek is a part; there's no law which says she can't do as she pleases on her own land. I guess it's just bad luck that your ranges are watered by . . .'

The remainder of the sheriff's speech was drowned in a roar of abuse. Storey waited for silence, then continued:

'You heard what the sheriff said, the law can't help us. All right then, we must take the law into our own hands. Horseshoe must be taught a lesson. We're not paying for water.'

'You bet we're not,' Buchan shouted, coming to his feet. 'I've buried one of my men, murdered by Horseshoe. It's time we took guns over to Horseshoe and showed 'em plain we ain't taking this lying down. That Lomax gal sure thinks she can ride roughshod over the whole country.'

Storey added: 'We'll fight – that's what we'll do

– fight!' The crowd shouted approval, filling the hall with noise. Frowning, Matt Flint pushed to the front and mounted the platform. He held up his hands to check the uproar, then said:

'Fighting won't settle this—'

Ben Storey turned on him.

'Shut up, Flint! This isn't your concern – you've got no right to interfere.'

Flint looked at him with contempt, then deliberately put his hand into Storey's face, and pushed. Ben Storey went over the edge of the platform, arms waving wildly, to fall amongst the crowd. Someone laughed. Buchan roared:

'Damn you, Flint – keep out of this!' Flint ignored him.

'Listen to me,' he implored the crowded hall. 'It is every man's duty to prevent bloodshed. If you follow Storey, you'll be plunged into range war – and there's no telling where that will stop. Horseshoe is a big outfit, bigger than the rest of yuh put together – and Berry has hired professional gunmen. You know what that means – in a straight fight, you won't have a chance. Some of you have wives and families to consider . . . you just can't afford to start a blood feud from which many of you would never return.'

Flint's sombre words silenced the men. He could see that he was swaying them, that he had effectually countered Storey's outburst. They were calculating chances now, and many of them

71

were uneasy. A voice from the back called:

'Well, what can we do? We aren't going to pay to water our cattle.'

Flint had been waiting for this, and he had the answer.

'I suggest that you form a cattleman's association. By acting together, legally, you'll be in a much stronger bargaining position. Further, I suggest that Sheriff Arnold be instructed to ride to Blue Rocks and put your case to the county marshal. The law must settle this dispute.'

Dan Hurst joined Flint on the platform.

'Matt's talking sense,' he said firmly. 'I'm backing his action all the way. Even the Horseshoe can't buck county law.'

Arnold added: 'I'm prepared to ride to Blue Rocks tonight, if the meeting decides to take Flint's advice.'

Several men started talking together, siding with Hurst. Then Ben Storey came back to the attack, shouting:

'That's all very fine, but how long will it take for the law to move? Berry said he'll start blasting tomorrow – by the time the law steps in, the river will have dried up and your herds perished. I say we can't afford to wait. We must act now, and that means—'

'That means innocent men are going to die, Ben Storey,' interrupted Nora Hurst in ringing tones. 'But not you! You talk big, but you won't be anywhere near the shooting. You'll be safe under cover, giving orders, while other men die!'

Storey went white with fury.

'You've no right to say that. I'm prepared to fight—' Jeers started at the back of the hall, drowning his voice.

'Nora's right – you've no guts, Ben! We're taking Flint's advice. Let the law settle with Horseshoe.' Hurst turned to the sheriff.

'You've got your orders, Arnold. The town wants the marshal of Blue Rocks in on this – and in a hurry.'

Sheriff Arnold nodded.

'I'll be riding fast,' he said, and made his way through the crowd, out of the hall to the street. He went direct to the stables to saddle his horse for the ride.

The meeting broke up after that, but it was Ben Storey who had the last word. He climbed back on the platform, bawling: 'You'll see – only guns will stop Horseshoe now!'

7

THE SNIPER

Dawn was a faint glimmer in the sky when Flint rose from his bed. He shaved and dressed and ate a hearty breakfast, left the hotel and made his way to the stable. Here, he saddled his roan, checked his Winchester and water canteen, and slung a bundle of provisions across the pommel.

He mounted and rode slowly out of town. Few saw him leave and none guessed his destination, which was the way Flint wanted it. He headed east, circling towards the Lazy S ranch. By the time he cleared the last straggling shacks, the sun was above the horizon, throwing red streaks through an early morning haze. Flint reckoned the day was going to be hot.

Out on the plain, he set the roan to a fast canter, cutting through brush and chaparral and skirting a belt of pine trees. He splashed through the river where it spread out over sand-banks, shallow and sluggish, and avoided the distant herds. The sun continued to rise and the sky became sparkling blue, cloudless, the air faintly stirring and warm with a dry heat.

An hour's riding brought Flint to the ranch-house. It was small and neatly laid out, two long wooden shacks set at right angles, the other two sides of the square formed by pole corrals. Nora Hurst came from the house at the sound of the roan's hoofs.

She regarded him with surprise, mingled with alarm.

'Has anything happened, Matt?' she asked.

Flint did not dismount.

'No, nothing new,' he replied. 'Dan around?'

'He's out with Mr Kincaid,' the girl said, 'down at the river. They're trying to construct some tanks, to hold water in case Sabina does block off the river. Just till the law settles things, that is.'

Flint nodded.

'Sensible attitude to take.' He paused, feeling for his pipe and filling it. 'I came to tell Dan I'm going up to Rimrock Creek. I figure that one man with a rifle can do a lot to hold up blasting operations—'

'Alone?' Nora said quickly.

'Yes. That's why I'm keeping the trip secret. I don't want Storey and Buchan horning in, sending men to start a shooting war. I can climb the cliffs above the gorge and shoot down on Berry's outfit, just enough to scare them off. Even with the sheriff riding hard, it's going to be several days before he gets back. I think I can hold up the dynamiting that long, and give the law a chance to act.'

'You're taking a big risk, Matt.'

'Someone has to do it,' Flint said quietly. 'Tell Dan where I've gone. I want him to keep Storey quiet till Arnold returns.'

'I'll tell him,' Nora promised.

Flint turned his horse to ride off. 'Be seeing yuh, Nora'

'Look after yourself, Matt . . .'

He waved back, settled himself in the saddle, and nudged the roan forward.

Away from the Lazy S, Flint rode easily, smoking his pipe and heading for the mountains. Another hour and he was on Horseshoe land; it gave him an odd feeling to be back on the range he had run for Piers Lomax. He knew the ground perfectly and was able to keep clear of outriders without trouble.

He rode in a wide arc, climbing steadily into the foothills towards Rimrock Creek. The prairie lay behind him; the country took on a more rugged aspect, mesquite and buffalo grass giving way to rock and cactus. The sun was hot and the air shimmered in waves.

Flint knew he was near the river by the rushing sound it made as it passed through the narrow gorge, but he did not come into the open. He wanted to surprise Berry's dynamiting gang.

He left his horse lower down, among the pines flanking the side of the rock slope, and proceeded on foot, carrying his rifle and provisions. He had to get above the river, to the heights looking down on the gorge.

It was a rough climb, tiring, but Flint was not the sort to give up easily. Higher and higher he dragged himself, methodically working towards a vantage point. There were boulders he had to go round, ledges that needed the greatest care to reach. And still he went up, into the blue sky, far above the cattle plains and the silver, winding river.

He reached the top at last and scrambled along the plateau to the cliff edge that looked sheerly down on the gorge. There was sloping ground for a few yards, and an outcrop of rock. Flint crawled into a hollow and made himself comfortable; he might be there a long time.

His water canteen he carefully placed out of the way of any bullets that might ricochet, and covered it over. A man can go quite a while without food, but not without water. Then he picked up his rifle, loaded it, and studied the gorge.

It was a narrow cleft in the rock face, some three hundred yards long, the sides sloping steeply. The river rushed through it, the dark swirling water piling high up the rock walls.

Upstream, a ledge ran along the inner wall of the gorge, and it was here that Berry's men must work.

Flint waited, nursing his rifle and watching the ledge; he would need to depend on his eyes, for he would not hear their approach above the noise of the river. The sun climbed higher and he shifted his position, taking advantage of the shade.

Twenty minutes passed before he saw tiny figures on the ledge far below. There were five of them, Sabina, slim and whiteshirted, her black hair uncovered; Berry, conspicuous by his fancy stetson; Calhoun, lumbering along like a huge bear; and two men carrying the dynamite and fuse-cord. They moved about, just above the level of the rushing water, with Berry looking for a place to set the first charge.

Still Flint waited. He was in no hurry; his plan was simply to gain time, to hold up operations until the sheriff got back from Blue Rocks. He had no intention of shooting to kill. Time was the important factor.

They had uncrated the sticks of dynamite and Berry was pointing up at a niche in the cliff face. Flint decided it was the moment to discourage them. He raised his Winchester, sighted carefully, and squeezed the trigger.

His shot echoed faintly. The shell sped down to the target, chipping splinters of rock from the wall-space between Berry and the man holding the dynamite. Reaction was instantaneous.

Berry spun round, clawing for his Colts and searching for the source of the shot. The other man threw his dynamite into the water; he didn't want to be holding that if another shot came. Sabina was staring at Berry as if he'd gone mad; she wouldn't have heard the shot over the sound of rushing water. Berry shouted something and Calhoun ran back along the ledge and disappeared from Flint's view. He returned, carrying a rifle.

Minutes ticked by with nothing much happening. Both sides waited; then Sabina grew impatient. She picked up another stick of dynamite and thrust it at the second man. Gingerly, he moved along the ledge to place the charge in position. Flint fired again, carefully.

His shot took the man's hat from his head. Calhoun's rifle erupted crimson flame and lead; puffs of smoke hung on the still air. His aim was wild, for he had not yet spotted Flint's position, and none of the bullets came close. All five figures retreated from the ledge.

Flint reached out and picked up the two empty cartridge cases ejected from his rifle; he placed them in line, on the floor of the hollow. He would need to keep a check on his ammunition for he might have to stay atop Rimrock Creek a couple of days. Berry and Calhoun, with the two hired gunmen, came back, all carrying rifles now. They lined up, some ten yards apart, and let loose a barrage of lead at the top of the gorge. Flint guessed they were firing blind, trying to scare him away. He kept low, not bothering to shoot back.

There was another lull. Berry and Sabina conversed, then Calhoun was given the job of placing a fresh charge while the other rifles covered him. Flint let Calhoun get into position before taking aim; the big man was climbing up the rock face to wedge the dynamite stick into a cranny. Flint fired, wounding Calhoun in the leg – he fell, missed the ledge and plunged into the river.

Flint saw his head bobbing in the water as he was carried downstream; then shells sprayed around him, ricocheting dangerously. The men below had his hiding place fixed now. He withdrew, content to let them waste shots.

Lead whined off the boulders about Flint, but he was well protected and remained unhit. He saw Calhoun crawl out of the water, a mile downstream; he did not appear to be seriously hurt.

After a while, Berry realized the futility of trying to shoot a man who remained under cover, high above him, and the firing stopped. They made another attempt to lay a charge. And again, Flint's rifle discouraged them.

Sabina stood on the ledge, waving her arms and shouting up at him. Flint thought he heard his name, but could not be sure. Likely, she was trying to buy him off. He did not bother to answer and all four retreated once more from the gorge.

Flint smiled a little, imagining Berry's rage. It would be evident to those below that they could not carry out their plans to dynamite Rimrock Creek, while a sniper controlled that exposed ledge. The next attempt would be on Flint himself.

He took a drink from his canteen and covered it over again; then he lay back, filled his pipe and smoked to pass away the time. The sun was scorching hot, baking the rocks about him, forcing him to move again, to seek new shade. Horseshoe land lay like a map below him; he could follow the course of the river for miles, see the distant blur of the ranch, dust rising from the herd of cattle.

Once, he had been foreman over all that he saw; now it was run by an outfit of gunmen – the thought made him sad. Sabina had a lot to answer for. He tilted his stetson forward to shade his eyes, and rested. He reckoned the time to be about noon, prepared himself a cold meal, and ate lei-surely.

A couple of hours passed before anyone showed on the ledge, then one man appeared, cautiously, dynamite in hand. It was a new face, and Flint guessed that Berry had called in reinforcements. He winged a shot downward and the man ran back.

Twice, at half-hour intervals, a man appeared, drawing Flint's fire. No serious attempt was made to lay a charge, so he knew this was only a decoy. They wanted to hold his attention while other men scaled the heights to attack him.

That didn't worry him; he had a strong position and was not likely to be driven off. The only thing he didn't like was not being able to see the men climbing up behind him; and he dare not leave the cliff edge for fear that those below would take their chance to dynamite the gorge. He could only wait.

Somewhere in the distance, upstream Matt judged, came the sound of an explosion. A second. A third. He sat up, watching, but seeing nothing. That would be the new channel they were blasting for the river to take; they had to look after Horseshoe's cattle. But that would remain ineffective until Rimrock Creek was blocked by hundreds of tons of rock.

Flint checked his Colt in case the enemy got near enough for him to use it. Again, he counted the row of used cartridges lined up on the floor of the hollow. Night would be the worst time; they'd try to creep up on him under cover of darkness.

Looking out over Horseshoe, Flint thought of Piers Lomax, remembering the manner of his death. His suspicions were roused again, not directed towards Ben Storey now, but at Reece Berry. Berry seemed to have taken charge of Horseshoe, using Sabina for his own ends. And it was Berry who had found Lomax's body on the range . . . Flint thought that circumstance would bear closer investigation.

But not just now. Someone was poking a stetson above the rocks, some twenty yards off; as it was unlikely that a head was under the hat, Flint refused to be drawn. He kept a sharp watch.

Down below, someone crawled along the ledge, carrying a stick of dynamite and a length of fusecord. Flint took aim and sent a shot downward; the man scurried back to safety.

Rifles exploded noisily nearby; Berry's gunmen knew his exact position now and were moving in, shooting as they came. Flint fired back as he saw a moving target. A man cried out, slipping down the steep rock face. Again a fusillade of shots came at Flint, chipping the rock and showering him with splinters; one piece struck his temple, drawing blood.

They ringed him in a half-circle, crouching behind boulders and firing steadily. Flint didn't think they'd try to rush him – there were ten yards of open ground separating them and he'd drop the first man to show himself. He located one of his attackers behind a moss-encrusted stone, and fired high, so that his shell ricocheted down. A man cursed, and bullets came winging back.

Down on the ledge by the river, another man tried to lay the charge that would block the gorge. Flint swivelled his Winchester round and let fly.

Reece Berry's voice sounded nearby: 'If that's

you holed up there, Flint, come out with your
hands above your head – or take what's coming to
you!'

Flint's reply was a lead slug in the direction of
Berry's voice. He heard a muttered, 'All right – let
him have it,' then followed a tense silence.

Flint shifted his position slightly, covering the
rocks with his rifle. Were they bluffing? Or
intending to rush him? He waited, grey eyes
narrowed over the barrel of his gun, jaw set and
grim. The firing had stopped completely and no
man showed himself. The rocky ledge below was
still deserted.

The end came suddenly – and, afterwards, Flint
blamed himself for not thinking of the obvious.
He'd been too sure they could not get near enough
to put him out of action, but he had underesti-
mated the cunning of Reece Berry. Flint had no
warning of what was coming.

He saw, too late, the small cylinder with sparks
glowing at one end. It was thrown high in the air,
to drop only a short distance from him . . . a stick
of dynamite with the fuse lit. It hit the ground,
exploded; and Flint had no time to act. There was
a short, brilliant flash of light; a roaring like thunder; and a blast of hot gases that sent him rocking
back on his heels. The ground shook under him
and small boulders were tossed into the air. He
had a vague impression of acrid black smoke
hanging over him, then one of the flying rocks

struck his head. He knew one moment of sharp agony before the black veils of unconsciousness swept over him.

Nora Hurst was worried. The time was late afternoon, the ranch-house of the Lazy S deserted. All the men were down at the river, working on the water tanks, and she had not seen her father to tell him of Flint's message.

She moved restlessly about the house, doing her chores, thinking of Flint, alone at Rimrock Creek. She could not keep her mind on what she was doing, for thinking about him. He might be in trouble – even dead. She put that thought out of her head.

Flint was well able to look after himself. He was strong and used to dealing with men of Reece Berry's breed. Nothing was going to happen to him, nothing could happen to him. She told herself this over and over, trying to get rid of her uneasiness. She left the house and went into the yard, turning to look up at the hills beyond Horseshoe. She listened hard. Was that gunshots she heard? Flint was alone – completely alone – against professional murderers. She bit her lip with worry.

Why, she asked herself, did she have to love Matthew Flint? Why couldn't she be content with a man who kept out of trouble? But it was that very quality, the instinct he had to stand up for what was right and honest, that had first attracted her to him. She knew that, and did not regret her choice.

He was stolid, almost clumsy in his deliberate ways, a man who took a pride in his work. Too rugged to be handsome, there was nothing flashy about Matt Flint; he was a true westerner, a man any woman could depend on. He was right now – she admitted that, even while she worried over him – right to make his stand against range war, to insist on bringing in the marshal from Blue Rocks, to try to prevent Horseshoe blocking the gorge without giving Ben Storey the chance to make more trouble.

He was right even to remain loyal to Sabina Lomax, though Nora had a struggle to admit that, even to herself. Sabina was beautiful, a natural magnet for men, and Nora was just a little jealous of a supposed attraction she held for Flint.

She thought of him at Rimrock Creek, alone; and knew that she would always love him, that no other man would ever satisfy her. She could not settle to her work while fears beset her.

Again, she thought she could hear distant gunfire, and could no longer bear the waiting. She wanted to be near the man she loved, to share his danger – and she made up her mind to go to him now, without delay.

Nora walked quickly back to the house, scribbled a note for her father, explaining the situation, and saddled her pony. She rode out of the ranch yard and headed for the hills beyond Horseshoe, taking a direct route; she had no fear of running into Berry's outfit, for Matt would be giving them plenty to think about.

She rode hard, her worries disappearing now that she was out on the range, doing something beside just waiting. She carried no gun and had little idea of purpose in her mind. That she might be a liability instead of an asset, to a man engaged in gun-battle, was something that simply did not occur to her. She was doing what was natural; going to the man she loved in his moment of danger.

The miles flashed by under her pony's flying hoofs. Rolling grassland gave way to rising ground covered with brush and stunted trees. The hills began. Ahead, shimmering in the heat haze, the line of mountains made a gaunt silhouette against a bright blue sky. She climbed higher, entering a belt of pines.

She was alone and the silence was timeless. No sound of gunfire reached her. Then, somewhere far off, from the direction of Rimrock Creek, came the muffled explosions of blasting operations. Nora's heart beat wildly. If Berry was dynamiting the gorge, it could only mean that Matt had failed, that he must be lying somewhere . . . she dare not finish the thought. She pressed on at greater speed.

Her pony was of Indian stock, sure-footed and having great stamina; the increasing ruggedness of the terrain made little difference to him. Nora followed the trail for Rimrock Creek, pushing her way between the solid trees on the hillside. Somewhere, not far off, a horse neighed softly. She stopped, wondering, friend or foe? And knew a moment of fear.

Then she advanced cautiously towards the sound, sliding from the saddle and moving up close on foot. She laughed; she had discovered Matt's roan, tethered in hiding. She brought her own pony to keep the roan company and set off up the steep slope.

Small noises warned her that others were approaching. She took cover, waiting to see who it was. Minutes passed, and a posse of men came down from the top of the gorge, Berry with Sabina, and four of the hired gunmen. She saw no sign of Flint. Berry's voice drifted to her as they passed:

'You're a vindictive puss, Sabina! I'd have shot Flint, not done that to him. Well, I suppose. . . .'

Nora heard no more for the riders moved on. There was coldness inside her. Something had happened to Matt! She hurried up the slope as fast as she could, panting from her exertions. Her pulse was thumping madly and she perspired freely. She clenched her hands till the nails dug into her skin. She prayed that she would be in time to save him.

The trees thinned out and she could see some distance ahead. There was a man amongst the trees; Calhoun. She went on with care. Suddenly, she saw Flint – and what they had done to him brought a cry of horror to her lips.

8

INDIAN TORTURE

Consciousness returned slowly to Matt Flint, bringing with it fresh pain. He could not think what was happening to him. His body received a constant succession of blows that jarred the breath from his lungs; his head was dazed, a blurred mist over his eyes.

Voices came faintly through the dull ache in his brain. The movements of men were all round him. His eyes opened, fought to understand the strangeness – the sky didn't seem to be in the right place, and trees leaned at odd angles. What he could see most of was bare rock and stunted thorn; these seemed to contain his whole world.

After a time, his memory began to function. He had been atop Rimrock Creek, fighting Berry's outfit, trying to stop them blasting the gorge. That much was clear – and he had failed. They had knocked him out by throwing dynamite; he was lucky to be still alive, he supposed, even if he were a prisoner. He wondered what they would do to him.

He was sufficiently aware of his surroundings now to understand what was happening. He was being dragged over rough ground, and the jolting he felt came from rocks and tree roots projecting above the surface. They must have dragged him like this, all the way down from the top of the gorge, for he saw that he was amongst trees, on the gentle slope of a hillside.

A woman's voice said: 'This will do,' and Flint came to rest, face down in the earth. He rolled over, sitting up, and spat dirt from his mouth.

Reece Berry laughed viciously. 'Go on, Flint,' he jeered. 'Try to make a break for it – I'm waiting!' He had a gun in his hand and looked as if he would enjoy using it.

Flint couldn't stand because there was a rope about his ankles and Calhoun was holding the other end. His gun-holster was empty, of course, and four armed men lounged just behind Berry. Even if Flint had felt strong enough to put up a fight, he wouldn't have stood much chance; as it was, he was content to lie on the ground and rest his aching body.

Sabina was present – Flint guessed that Berry had spared his life solely on her account – and she looked good and mad about something. She stood over him, black hair blowing free and her hands on her hips. She looked wild and beautiful and full of menace.

'Matthew Flint,' she said in a hard voice. 'You've interfered in my plans once too often. This time you're going to be taught a lesson. Reece was for killing you outright, but I've a better idea. You're going to suffer. . . .'

She turned to the gunmen, and snapped:

'I want two ropes, one over a high branch of each of those two trees.' She pointed at two young fines some ten feet apart. 'See to it – and Calhoun, release his feet.'

Calhoun bent over him, and Flint had a close-up of the big man's ugly face, scarred and twisted and horrible. Calhoun slashed at the rope with a long knife, not worrying when he cut into Flint's flesh. Flint stretched his legs, trying to get some life back into them.

He watched as two men looped ropes over the pine branches. An idea formed at the back of his mind, but he rejected it. Not even Sabina could contemplate that.

Berry lit a cigarette, one-handed. There was a cruel smile on his handsome face and his eyes were alert for any movement on Flint's part. He kept his Colt levelled.

Calhoun said: 'What yuh going to do with him, Miss Lomax?'

Sabina laughed shortly.

'I saw this done once, by the Indians. Flint isn't going to like it. All right, bring him over here – and tie one end of each rope to his wrists. Make a good job of it because the knots will have to take a strain.'

Flint climbed to his feet, hobbling with pain. He swayed from weakness – no good trying to run for it. Two men closed in on him, dragged him to a spot central between the pines, and secured a rope to each wrist. Berry dug his gun into Flint's back, and hissed:

'Just try something – I'd like the pleasure of emptying my gun into your kidneys!'

Flint stood still, looking at the girl. He said:

'Think what you're doing, Sabina – you don't want to do anything you'll regret later on. What would your father have said about this? He—'

Calhoun swung his fist into Flint's mouth, and snarled:

'Shut up!'

The ugly man was limping as a result of his leg wound. The ropes were pulled tight, lifting Flint's arms above his head.

'Higher,' Sabina shouted. 'Take him up higher!'

The men on the ropes pulled harder. Flint felt his feet leave the ground, the weight of his body taken on his arms. The rope cut into his wrists and he had to bite his lip to check a cry of pain.

'Enough,' Sabina said suddenly. 'Let him rest

93

with his toes touching the ground – then make the ropes fast to the tree trunks.'

Berry was grinning. He holstered his gun and tossed away his cigarette butt.

'That's fine,' he said. 'Flint is sure going to get tired of balancing on his toes that way. I reckon the Indians knew a thing or two about torture! A few hours in that position will cripple him for life.'

The ropes were secured in place. Sabina said: 'Let's get down to the gorge, there's still enough light to set the first charge. I'd like Flint to hear that before he faints.'

She untethered her horse and swung into the saddle. 'Maybe I'll come back and cut you down,' she said softly, 'if I don't forget!'

Berry and the other men mounted and followed after her. Calhoun looked at Berry, who nodded, and the ugly man's face moved in silent laughter. He drew his gun and sat on a tree stump near Flint; when he got tired of watching Flint's agony, he would use his gun. Berry was taking no chances of Sabina changing her mind. . . .

Matt Flint's face ran with sweat. His muscles ached from the strain of his unnatural position. With each movement of the pines in the breeze, his toes left the ground. He fought for balance, trying to keep his feet supporting his weight, taking the strain off his arms. He knew that before long his body would go numb, that he would lose consciousness.

He hung there, arms angled out above his head, the ropes from his wrists looped over the pine branches and tied down. Only his toes touched the ground. With every minute, he could feel the strain increasing.

Calhoun left the tree stump and came towards him.

'Like it?' he asked, and pushed Flint's chest roughly.

Flint swung in the air, kicking out. Calhoun laughed.

'Just in case yuh get the idea you're going to be cut down,' he growled, 'let me tell yuh I aim to get a little target practice later on — with you as the target! But there's no hurry. You can swing a while longer yet ... Reece wouldn't want the Lomax gal to hear shooting.'

Flint got his toes back on the ground, strained with his legs, stretching his body to give his arms a rest. The muscles of his calves and thighs began to ache; he sagged, and the ropes bit into his wrists again.

Calhoun sat on the log and rolled himself a cigarette. He smoked at leisure, taking a keen interest in Flint's torture. Every few seconds he would laugh or make some jeering remark. Then he would take out his Colt, spin the chambers, point the muzzle carefully at Flint — and put it back in his holster, grinning.

The minutes passed with a dreadful slowness.

Flint's head rolled forward; his neck felt as if it were supporting a leaden ball, too heavy to hold. He forced his head back, but had to let it fall again. A breeze stirred the trees, lifting his feet clear of the ground. He fought to maintain balance, sweating profusely, agony in every limb.

He knew he could not hold out for long. Already, his awareness was fading. Calhoun got to his feet, walked up to Flint and pushed him so that he swung in the air. It felt as if his arms were being wrenched from their sockets.

Calhoun said: 'I guess Sabina is far enough off not to hear gunshots. This is the end of the trail for you, Flint. I'm going to sink lead into yuh!'

He walked back a few paces, stood with feet apart, half crouching, gun at his waist. Flint spoke a brief prayer, for it seemed to him that his last moment had come; he could do nothing to help himself. The killer light showed in Calhoun's pig eyes; he took aim . . .

Matt Flint felt nothing. Waiting for death, he knew complete numbness; even the pain in his arms and legs faded to a dull monotony. The ground might have been miles beneath him. He heard a feminine voice – 'Stop!'

Calhoun spun round, gun in hand, angry. Flint thought: Sabina's come back. His eyes fought to stay open, and saw a slim figure in riding clothes. Not Sabina Lomax – Nora Hurst.

He roused himself, and shouted: 'Nora, go back!

Get away!' Then the strain on his arms became too much to bear; his whole body went slack and his head dropped across his chest. Nora walked up to Calhoun, keeping her gaze on his ugly face.

'You daren't shoot a woman,' she said calmly. 'The west wouldn't be big enough to hide you.'

Calhoun hesitated, knowing she was right. A man who harmed a woman would be hunted down and killed without mercy; that was an unwritten law of the west. He put his gun away – he didn't need it anyway. She was only a slip of a girl – but pretty, he thought, very pretty. And they were alone.

He had a different light in his eyes when he advanced on her, arms reaching out to seize her.

'You're going to kiss me,' he told her. 'There ain't no one to stop us here.'

Nora backed away. She was scared, but quite calm. She had to save Matt, that was the thought in her head. She had to get Calhoun out of the way somehow.

He was coming after her, lumbering like a giant bear, his ugly face twisted in a smile. His breath stank.

'Stand still,' Calhoun snarled suddenly. 'Damn yuh, don't keep moving away. I ain't going to hurt yuh.'

He knew that women shunned him because of his face – and this one was going to make up for the insults he'd had to stand. He was going to hold her in his arms and kiss her. He started forward again, making a rush for her.

Nora stood still, perfectly balanced, waiting. This was what she wanted, to get him moving at speed. She was stronger than she looked, and knew how to take care of herself. She let Calhoun almost touch her, then darted under his arms and seized him round the waist. His momentum carried him on, and, with one deft movement, Nora threw him over her shoulders. He landed heavily, his head crashing against the hard, rock ground, stunning him. He lay there, unconscious, a surprised look on his face.

She stooped over him and took the knife at his belt. Then she ran to Flint and cut him down. He dropped in a heap, unmoving. She tried to lift him, but he was a dead weight in her arms.

For a moment, she despaired. Flint was badly hurt and it was unlikely he would be able to walk for some hours after he regained consciousness. The night was coming on. And Berry might return.

She made up her mind, took Calhoun's gun with her, and ran down the hillside. She kept going at full speed till she came to the place where she had left her pony and Flint's big bay roan. Speed was essential; she didn't know how long Calhoun would stay unconscious, and she didn't want to face him again.

She freed the horses, mounted her pony and led

Flint's horse back up the hill. There was a burning hatred in her; Sabina had done this thing to Matt – no man could be so cruel. She would have liked to get her hands on Sabina Lomax at that moment.

Back at the pines, both Flint and Calhoun lay as she had left them, neither man stirring. She led the roan up to Flint's body, stripped off the saddle, and started to lift him on to the horse's back. It was a difficult job for her, for Flint was a big man, and heavy; but she got his shoulders up, then heaved him over.

He wouldn't stay there on his own, so she used a rope to lash him in position. All the time, she worried over Calhoun coming to, and cursed Sabina.

He was secure at last. Nora mounted the pony and took the reins of Flint's horse and set off down the hill. Matt needed treatment, that was obvious; she'd take him to the Lazy S, then ride to Rimrock for the doctor.

9
ALIBI

Matt Flint was confined to bed for several days after his experience at Rimrock Creek. The doctor came daily to visit him, bringing news from town, and Nora nursed him. Flint lay on his back and listened as first one person brought news of the outside world, then another – and all of it bad. Slim, grey-haired, Dan Hurst sat by Flint's bedside and worried over the sheriff's prolonged absence.

'If Arnold doesn't come back soon, I don't know what's going to happen,' he said. 'Horseshoe have near enough blocked the creek and there's only a trickle of water getting through to the other ranges. All hell is due to bust loose before long.'

Then there was the doctor, fresh from town. He was small, with a pointed beard and brisk manner.

'Horseshoe have gunmen patrolling the border of their range; strangers just aren't wanted over there. Bill Yates and some of the Double U boys had a skirmish with them. A lot of lead flew but fortunately no one was seriously hurt – it looks as though I'll be having a lot of work if the situation doesn't improve.'

Kincaid drifted in, pushed his hat to the back of his head and dropped into a chair. He made himself a smoke, and said:

'Guess what, Matt? I ran into the preacher this morning; yesterday, he was out at Horseshoe. Berry and Sabina are married, man and wife. What d'yuh reckon to that?'

The tall man's long jaw and sad eyes revealed what he felt about it, and Flint sympathised.

'Sure sorry to hear that, Kincaid, but you've got one consolation – likely she'll be a widow before long!'

Flint's thoughts flew to Sabina, and his manner grew sombre. It seemed to him that Berry was set to take over the Horseshoe himself. If anything should happen to Sabina. . . .

'You can do something to help, though. I'd do it myself if I could move faster than a crawl; it's this – I want you to snoop around town. Someone there must be giving Berry an alibi for the time of Lomax's death . . . I want to know who that someone is. This is really the sheriff's job, but seeing he's out of town, I want you to do it. Don't go stirring up trouble. Just come back here and report what yuh learn. That clear?'

101

Kincaid nodded, picked up his hat and went to the door.

'I'll do it, Matt.'

The next caller was Inigo Webb. He'd come to talk to Dan Hurst, but Hurst was busy on the range.

'Ben Storey's dead,' he informed Flint. 'Ben drove his cattle onto Horseshoe land, trying to get them to water. There was a fight and Ben got shot. Buchan's scared; he talks big but he doesn't do anything. I guess it's up to me and Dan to fight Horseshoe – it's that, or go under. Horseshoe is boss of the range now, and Berry and the Lomax gal sure let us know it.'

After Webb had left, Flint packed his pipe and smoked, staring at the ceiling. He had plenty to think about. With Storey dead, the threat of a range war fizzled out; but now Horseshoe was in a position to give orders and make them stick. The small ranchers needed their water badly – and Horseshoe alone had access to the new course of the river. He did not know which was worse.

Sabina worried him. She seemed completely in Berry's power, and Flint could guess what would happen when he tired of her. There would be another 'accident'.

Kincaid returned from Rimrock.

'The man you want is called Johns,' he told Flint, 'and he runs a saloon called the Silver Spur, though to look at the place I'd say the silver had got kinda tarnished. It's a filthy hole. Johns is a card-sharp, crooked as they come. According to him, Berry was there when Lomax took his fall – it wasn't till some time afterwards that he discovered Lomax's body. He didn't have any answer when I asked what Berry was doing on Horseshoe land.'

Flint thought that over, his suspicions growing. Lomax's death had come just right for Reece Berry to walk into Horseshoe. He remembered Johns vaguely, though the Silver Spur was not the sort of saloon he frequented. A tall, dark-skinned *hombre* with long sideboards and slender hands; a flashy sort of individual.

Kincaid said, interrupting his thoughts:

'If Berry got at Lomax somehow—'

'It's just an idea,' Flint said sharply, 'so keep it to yourself. Suspicions aren't proof.'

He lay awhile, thinking over what he should do, and becoming increasingly restless. Flint was not a man used to spending days on his back; he felt the need for action. The whole set-up revolved about Reece Berry – get rid of Berry, and Sabina would come to her senses. And the way to get at Berry was through the gambler, Johns.

Abruptly, Flint threw off the bed-clothes and swung his feet to the floor. He stood up, weak and unsteady. He tested his arms and legs; he could walk and swing his arms. What he needed, he decided, was exercise.

He dressed and shaved, borrowed one of

Hurst's .45's and went outside. It was afternoon, hot under a blazing sun; he thought grimly of what the heat might do to cattle short of water. The ranch seemed deserted. He went to the stable, saddled his roan and led the horse into the yard.

Nora came running up.

'Matt! What are you doing out of bed? The doctor said—'

Flint grinned.

'I'm obliged to the doctor for his consideration, but I've a job to finish. Don't worry, Nora, I feel fine. A ride on the range and a breath of fresh air will do me more good than lying abed. 'Sides, there's a man I want to talk to in Rimrock.'

Nora Hurst looked anxiously at him.

'You're in no shape to go hunting trouble, Matthew Flint,' she snapped. 'I didn't go to all the trouble I did to save your life, just to have you ride off and get killed now!'

Flint became serious.

'I'm thanking yuh for saving my life, Nora. It was a brave thing you did, riding to Rimrock Creek alone, and I'm not forgetting I wouldn't be here now but for you. But I'm a man built for action, not hiding behind a woman's skirts. There's big trouble brewing, and I think I see a way to stop it. I'll be coming back, don't fret.'

He looked down at her, saw the beauty in her, the appeal in her brown eyes. He took a step closer, and said, softly:

'Nora, I want yuh to know that I love you. When this business is finished, I'll be asking you to marry me.'

Her eyes shone moistly, and she lifted her lips for him, waiting. Flint gathered her in his arms and kissed her, holding her close to his chest and feeling the warmth of her.

She whispered: 'I love you, Matt. Hurry back – I'll be waiting.' He released her, mounted the roan and cantered away. Her voice followed him out of the yard, fading:

'Look after yourself, Matt. Be careful, for my sake!'

Flint waved back, then rode out to the prairie. The grass was turning brown, wilting under a scorching sun. He went down to the river, halted a moment, frowned at the dried mud. There was a trickle of water in the bed, no more. The cattle were in for a bad time unless something was soon done.

He rode on, making fair speed for Rimrock. The gentle motion of his horse and the wind on his face made him feel better; he forgot he had just risen from a sick-bed, and became a man craving physical action.

The town was quiet. Dogs slept in the shade, a few women talked on street corners; there were no men about except those in the stores. All the punchers were out on the plains, hard pressed with thirsty steers to handle.

Flint avoided the doctor's house and trotted slowly along the length of Main Street. He passed the sheriff's office, closed, and knew that Arnold had not yet returned from Blue Rocks. He went on to the far side of town, to the shanties and the Silver Spur Saloon.

Here, he dismounted, tethered his horse and hitched up his gun-belt. He let his right hand caress the butt of his borrowed .45 before he went through the batwing doors. The saloon was empty except for the proprietor. Johns sat at a table, alone, turning up cards in a slick, professional manner and shuffling them skilfully.

The gambler shifted a brown cheroot from the corner of his mouth and spoke.

'Drink or a game? Or maybe both?'

Flint swept the cards from the table and said, harshly:

'Neither. I'm here for information.'

Johns pushed back his chair and came to his feet, a sullen anger in his face.

'Who the hell d'yuh think you are?' he demanded.

Flint stepped in and slapped his hand across the gambler's face, knocking the cheroot from his mouth and sending a shower of sparks to the floor.

He said: 'You know damn well who I am – Matthew Flint! Reece Berry was supposed to be here when Lomax died. I want the truth about that, and you're going to tell me.'

Johns took a step back, rubbing his hand over his mouth.

'Don't know what you're talking about,' he mumbled.

Flint let his eyes leave Johns and move about the saloon. The place was badly kept; the mirror was thick with dust, the sawdust on the floor filthy and smelling of stale liquor.

'A nice rat-hole,' he said coldly. 'The sort of place I'd expect to find Berry's friends.'

Johns didn't speak. There was a wariness in his eyes, mixed up with hatred. And he was a coward . . . he made no move to draw the short-barrelled Derringer in the shoulder holster under his open jacket. He stood before Flint, tall and greasy, his long hands moving jerkily.

Flint hit him in the belly, driving him back to the wall.

'Lost yore tongue, *hombre*? You know what I want to hear – start talking!'

He followed up, took the Derringer away from him and threw it across the room.

Johns said: 'I'll have the law on yuh, Flint, assaulting a man and threatening him.'

Flint laughed.

'The sheriff's out of town, and Berry is too busy with Horseshoe to worry over the likes of you. This is just between the two of us, Johns, make up your mind to that.'

107

'What d'yuh want to know?'

Flint's grey eyes bored into the gambler.

'Just tell me where Reece Berry was and what he was doing at the time of Lomax's death.'

Johns forced a smile.

'Seems to me you've heard already' he replied. 'Reece was here with me, playing cards. He found Lomax's body by chance after he left here, long after Lomax took his fall.'

'The two of yuh were alone?' Flint demanded. 'There's no one else to back your word?'

'Isn't my word good enough then? We were alone, and you can't prove otherwise.'

Flint spat: 'You're lying, Johns. Berry murdered Piers Lomax and paid you to alibi him.'

Johns laughed wildly.

'Prove it! Just try to prove it, Flint!'

'Maybe I'm not interested in proof,' Flint said drily. 'Lomax was a good friend to me – maybe I'll take the law into my own hands and avenge his death. Starting with you . . .'

The gambler's face lost colour.

'You wouldn't kill me in cold blood, Flint! Not even you could get away with that.'

'Berry seems to,' Flint drawled. 'Maybe I can find somebody to say I was elsewhere, too.'

'You're bluffing. Well, you can't make me talk. I'll tell Reece about this – he'll know how to handle you.'

'He's tried,' Flint pointed out, 'and failed.'

He turned and walked across the room, picked up a lamp and smashed it on the floor. Oil leaked out and ran over the boards. He swept a pile of sawdust and old papers onto the oil, struck a match and dropped it to the floor. The paper caught fire, spreadlng hungrily through the trail of oil. The wood began to crackle fiercely.

Johns cursed.

'Damn you, Flint – you can't do this! I'll have the law on yuh.'

He threw himself at Flint, fists flailing. Flint dodged, and sank one blow into the gambler's face, flooring him.

The blaze caught, dry wood burning furiously. In minutes, there would he no trace of the Silver Spur. Dense black smoke filled the room.

Coughing, Flint dragged Johns to the door and pitched him face down in the dirt.

'Get out of town,' he told the gambler. 'Your sort aren't wanted in Rimrock. Show yore face here again, and I'll come gunning for yuh!'

Swearing angrily, Johns ran for his horse. He swung into the saddle and rode off.

Men came running as the fire spread. Buckets of water were passed along a chain; no one thought of trying to save the Silver Spur, only of preventing the blaze from spreading.

'What happened to Johns?' someone in the crowd asked.

To which, Flint drawled: 'I reckon he got the

idea it wasn't healthy for him round these parts.' Though the saloon was gutted, the fire had been kept under control. There was no danger to the rest of the town.

Matt Flint went for his roan, climbed stiffly into the saddle and jogged out of town. He was feeling pleased with himself. Johns was yellow and he was going straight to Reece Berry for help. And Flint wanted to be there when they met.

He set his horse at the gallop till he picked up Johns' trail, then eased his pace. He didn't want the gambler to guess he had been deliberately panicked into running so that Flint could follow him.

The shadows were lengthening as the sun sank to the horizon. Night darkness would be swift in coming. Matthew Flint rode on, following after Johns, knowing this was the beginning of the showdown.

10
THE MURDERER

Away from the lights of Rimrock, dusk settled a grey shroud over the prairie. Night clouds gathered and the stars gave a fitful light. There was a slight wind, blowing into Flint's face and carrying the sound of Johns' horse. Occasionally, he caught a glimpse of his quarry, far ahead.

Johns was riding fast, heading straight for Horseshoe territory, and Flint kept well back, content to stalk his man without being seen. The ground sloped gently through the darkness, down to the river bed, now dry mud and rock, with a few pools of stagnant water.

Flint became wary, for they were on Horseshoe land, and he could expect to encounter Berry's riders before long. He wanted to avoid a fight if possible; it was more important for him to overhear what passed between Johns and Berry.

In the distance, cattle lowed. The Horseshoe

herd was not far off. The splashing noise of water came to him through the night and he knew that he was near the new course of the river. There would be armed men on patrol here.

The sky was black, clouded over, with only a few stars showing to give faint light to the landscape. Flint reined back his horse, moving slowly and cautiously. A pine, tall and ghostly, loomed out of the darkness; a coyote howled to its mate; the smell of juniper drifted to him.

A voice hailed Johns and the gambler stopped, answering. Flint moved in closer, straining his ears to catch the conversation.

He heard his own name mentioned, then — 'Lend me a gun, will yuh?' Johns said. 'I didn't have time to stop and pick one up.' He got his gun. 'Where's Reece? I've got to talk with him, pronto.'

'Berry's down river aways,' came the reply. 'Head south and you'll find him all right.'

Johns rode off again, and, circling to miss the guards, Flint followed him. The water was a broad stream, flowing between grassy dunes, shallow and shining in the starlight. The Horseshoe cattle made a dark, shifting mass along the river. There were trees now, pine and cottonwood, growing close together, and Flint was able to get nearer to the gambler without revealing himself.

Johns stopped again, and Flint saw that he had come upon Reece Berry. Calhoun was with him. They sat on their horses, bunched together, talking. Flint slipped from the saddle and left the roan's reins trailing the ground. He crept up on foot.

Johns was speaking: 'That – Flint came after me and burnt down the Silver Spur. He told me to get out of town. He's onto yuh, Berry – you know about what. I've got to talk to you, private.'

Berry laughed unpleasantly.

'You always were a yellow rat, Johns! Don't let Flint worry you – I'll take care of him.'

Johns said, sullenly: 'You want me to talk in front of Calhoun?'

There was a pause, then Berry spoke again.

'Calhoun, ride down the river apiece. See that the men are on their toes. I don't want anybody watering his cattle on Horseshoe land. Get moving!'

The ugly man turned his stallion and rode away, heading almost straight for the place where Flint was hiding. Flint dropped flat on the ground, hugging cover. Calhoun passed within a few yards without seeing him, and went on.

Berry turned savagely on the gambler.

'If you've opened yore mouth to Flint, by God, I'll—'

Johns said, hurriedly: 'I didn't tell the man anything, Reece, honest I didn't. But he suspects something. I'm warning yuh, Matt Flint is no man to play around with. He's tough.'

Berry swore loudly.

'I'll see him to hell before he's much older! Is that all you've got to say?'

'No.' Flint crept stealthily nearer. Johns' voice came clearly to him through the gloom. 'Don't forget I know what happened to Lomax – you roped his horse so he took a fall, then, while he was unconscious, cracked his skull with a rock.'

'Not so loud, you fool,' Berry burst out angrily. 'You've been well-paid to keep your mouth shut. Keep it that way, or I'll shut it permanently.'

'I've got to clear out,' Johns said. 'And I reckon it's up to you to make good the loss of the Silver Spur. That's why I'm here, to collect!'

'If you think—'

The gambler turned suddenly.

'I thought I heard someone move. Over there, by the trees.'

Flint caught his breath, fumbling for his Colt. Berry peered into the darkness, said:

'There's no one. You've got bad nerves, that's all.'

He turned back to Johns, then exploded violently:

'You double-crossing rat! Pull a gun on me while my back's turned – I'll. . . .'

The gambler said, harshly: 'You won't do anything except hand over your wallet. Then I'm clearing out of these parts for good. Don't try to draw – you're covered and my trigger-finger's itching. You owe me plenty, Berry, for covering up a murder, but I haven't time to bleed yuh. I'll just take what you're carrying, and ride. Hand it over!'

Flint smiled to himself. Neither man trusted the other; Berry would have killed Johns, just to keep his mouth shut – and the gambler only felt safe while he had a gun in his hand. They were a fine pair.

Berry dipped his hand in his shirt pocket and brought out a roll of notes. He tossed them at Johns, and said, contemptuously:

'Now clear out. If I meet you again, I'll shoot yuh down like the rat you are!'

The gambler flipped through the notes, counting.

'Only five hundred bucks. If I had the time . . .' he checked himself, thrusting the money into his pocket. 'Don't worry, Reece, yuh won't be seeing me again. I don't aim to hang around and have Flint jump me a second time.'

He gestured with his gun.

'Get off yore horse.'

Berry obeyed. Johns slashed the animal's rump with his hat, driving it off. 'Now throw your guns away – carefully, mind!'

Berry hesitated, then drew one Colt and tossed it into the darkness. He threw the other after it.

Johns chuckled. 'That'll do. *Adios*, Reece!'

He wheeled his horse, used the spurs, and was away at a gallop. Berry dived for his guns, but the gambler had disappeared into the night by the

115

time he got them. Cursing, he went after his horse.

Flint was already moving for his roan. Berry could wait – it was Johns he wanted – in the witness box, retelling the story of Lomax's death before a jury. He mounted swiftly and headed in the direction the gambler had taken.

It was some minutes before he picked up the sound of thudding hoofs ahead, then the clouds parted and starlight revealed a horseman silhouetted against the horizon. Berry had not given chase, and Johns was swerving away from the wer, heading for the desert and the border beyond.

Flint urged the roan to speed and gave his horse its head. There was little danger of running into Horseshoe riders now; it was between him and Johns alone. The roan stretched itself to the limit, covering the ground at a great pace. The distance between them shortened. The chase was nearing its end.

Flint, crouched in the saddle and leaning forward against his mount's neck, uncoiled his lariat for the throw. Dark clouds obscured his view. He swept on, past tapering pines and through short scrub – then the stars shone again, clearly revealing the quarry.

He cast his noose, watching it settle over Johns' shoulders, and reined to a halt. His saddle-horn took the strain as the gambler was dragged from

116

his horse to the ground. Johns gave one cry as he rolled in the dirt, then the breath was knocked out of him.

Flint rode slowly up, coiling in the lariat. He had his .45 in his hand when he reached Johns.

'All right, feller,' he said quietly. 'On your feet.'

Johns staggered upright, gasping for breath, his eyes watering.

'Damn you, Reece,' he exclaimed. 'Why can't yuh—'

Flint interrupted: 'I'm not Reece Berry, for which you can think yourself darned lucky. He'd have used a gun to drop yuh, not a rope.'

Johns stood panting, his face marked from the fall. He didn't look flashy now, just scared.

'So it's you, Flint,' he muttered. 'How in hell did you get here?'

'I followed yuh from Rimrock. That was a mighty interesting talk you had with Berry.'

Fear flickered behind Johns' eyes. His lean body tensed and he caught his breath.

'You can't prove anything. I'll deny it. It's only your word against mine and—'

'And I reckon the sheriff will take my word,' Flint finished drily. 'You'll talk all right – to save yore neck! Rimrock folk won't take kindly to your covering up for a murderer. You'll talk fast enough, and Reece Berry will swing.'

He hooked Johns' gun from its holster and thrust it into his belt.

117

'Now get back on your horse. I'm taking yuh in to Rimrock, where you'll stay in gaol till the sheriff returns from Blue Rocks.' Awkwardly, because Flint still had his rope on him, the gambler climbed back in the saddle. Flint set his roan at a canter, leading the other horse. Johns didn't open his mouth again; he realized the position he was in and didn't like it. He was trapped between Flint and Berry, and neither man was going to spare him.

Flint swung in an arc to avoid the river and Berry's patrol, then headed straight for Rimrock. The night was still young when he arrived back in town; lights shone from saloon windows and a piano tinkled. There were few people about and little noise. Rimrock had nothing to celebrate at the moment.

There was still no light in the sheriff's office so Flint knew that Arnold had not returned. He dismounted and hitched his horse, dragging Johns up the boardwalk. Someone was waiting in the shadows.

'I knew you'd be back, Matt,' said a breathless feminine voice.

'Nora! What are you doing here?'

'I had to come. Something might have happened to you.'

Flint opened the door of the law office, pushed Johns inside and went in. Nora followed him, closing the door as he lit a lamp.

118

Flint said: 'Nothing happened to me, but plenty is going to happen to Reece Berry. Johns here, is going into the witness box to convict him of the murder of Piers Lomax!'

Nora was silent for so long that Flint turned to look at her. She was gazing at him with an intent expression on her face.

'And Sabina?' she asked finally.

Flint shrugged.

'Sabina will have to take what comes to her. She joined Berry of her own free will.'

He pushed Johns through the rear door of the law office, to the passage leading to the cells behind. He locked him in the first cell and slipped the key in his pocket.

'I'll talk,' the gambler said. 'I'll tell the truth about Reece killing Lomax. All I ask is, don't let Berry get at me!'

Flint replied shortly: 'You can talk to the sheriff. He'll decide the rest.'

He walked back to the office, where Nora waited for him.

'What now, Matt?' she asked.

Flint sat at Arnold's desk and filled his pipe with slow deliberation. He struck a match and lit up, waving away smoke with a large hand. A worried expression formed on his face.

'Sabina-' he said, and paused.

It was not so easy for him to dismiss Sabina from his thoughts. He had promised Lomax to look out for her, and she was in bad trouble. He thought: Does she really love Reece Berry? How was she going to take the news that he killed her father? And now she was married to him. . . .

Nora said nothing. She watched Matt Flint anxiously, knowing she could do nothing to resolve the conflict in his mind. This was something he had to settle himself.

Flint spoke. 'Obviously, Berry is only after the Horseshoe. He killed Lomax for that end. And he married Sabina simply to get a legal claim on the ranch – that means Sabina is in great danger. She must be warned.'

He rose, pacing the room, puffing smoke from his pipe. 'I'll ride out and see her tonight.'

Nora said, bitterly: 'Must it be you who always takes the risk, Matt? Can't you leave it for the sheriff?'

Flint shook his head.

'I promised Lomax-'

'I know! And you can't break a promise . . . are you forgetting Sabina tried to knife you in the back? And that she had you strung up between those trees?'

'I'm not forgetting,' Flint said grimly. 'But I'm going, just the same.'

Nora sighed.

'I wish you weren't,' she said wistfully.

Flint went to the door.

'This trouble will be over when Sabina gets rid

of Reece Berry. She'll come to her senses – and your father will get water for his herd. Don't you see, Nora? I must ride to the Horseshoe.'

She did not answer. Flint went out, mounted his roan and headed out of town. Neither he nor Nora saw the shadowy figure lurking in a doorway across the street. This man, too, mounted his horse and left town; he did not follow Flint, but headed for the river to find Reece Berry. Berry would be interested in learning that Flint had Johns in gaol.

11

NEWS TRAVELS FAST

The moon came up, bathing the prairie in a silver glow, while Flint was barely half way to the Horseshoe. He rode fast, heading straight for the ranch, except for a minor detour to avoid the watchers by the river. He had no wish to think of the embarrassing meeting ahead; it was an unpleasant chore, but one that must be done. So he rode at the gallop to keep his thoughts away from Sabina Lomax.

He reached the knoll overlooking the ranch buildings, and reined to a halt. Berry and most of the men would be down by the river; even so, Flint did not want to move rashly. He wanted Sabina alone when he talked with her.

Moonlight was bright, revealing the big house standing in the shadow of a lone pine; he could even make out the form of Lomax's grave. A light showed in the house; none in the riders' log cabin. Flint rode down the slope to the patio, moving slowly to avoid making a noise.

He left his roan untethered, for a quick getaway if trouble should start, and mounted the steps to the house. There seemed no one about. Quickly, he stepped through the door and went along the passage to the living room. The door was half open, and, through it, he saw the girl.

She sat hunched in a big chair, staring down at the pumaskin rug at her feet, brooding. The light of the single oil-lamp standing on the rough pine table showed that she was alone in the room. She was dressed for riding, in a man's shirt and leather skirt, and a small flat crowned stetson lay on the table.

Unobserved, Flint stood in the doorway, watching her. Her complexion seemed wan, her whole pose listless. She was still beautiful to look upon, but some of the wildness had gone. Flint formed the impression that she was miserable, and wondered if she were beginning to suspect the truth about Reece Berry.

He entered the room, and said, casually:

'Hello, Sabina.'

She started abruptly, half-rising, with an eagerness flushing her face.

'Is that you, Reece?'

Then the girl recognized him, and her whole

123

manner changed. She became taut, on the defensive. Her voice assumed a harshness.

'What do you want here, Flint?'

He advanced towards her, closing the door and keeping away from the line of the window.

'Just a few words, Sabina. Sit down again – I'm not here to harm you.'

She sat down, but did not relax; her dark eyes were intent on him, wary and watchful.

'If you're looking for Reece,' she snapped, 'he's not here. I'm quite alone, and you needn't think I'm afraid of you, either!'

Flint perched himself on the edge of the table. He said, mildly: 'There's no need for you to be afraid of me. I'm here to warn you-'

'Against Reece, I suppose?'

Flint nodded. Sabina laughed softly.

'Then you needn't bother. Since I married him, I've found out he's – different – from the man I thought him. But don't think that makes any difference. I still love him, and always will!'

There was a note of defiance in her voice, but it went immediately. In a changed tone, she added:

'You were right, Matt. I have regretted what I did to you at Rimrock Creek. I'm glad your escaped. I want you to know I'm sorry about that.'

Flint waited for her to go on, but she did not speak again. He stared about the room, wishing he were anywhere else, that it was somebody else who must break this news.

'What I have to say isn't easy, Sabina.' He paused: there didn't seem to be any way round the subject – he had to plunge straight in. 'Reece Berry murdered your father. . . .'

The girl came out of her chair like a tigress, pale and tense; her eyes flashing.

'You dirty liar!' she hissed. 'Take that back before I kill you.'

Flint slid off the table and stood prepared to defend himself. He tried to remain calm as he continued:

'Berry killed your father by roping his horse, then cracking his skull while he lay unconscious on the ground – that's the sort of man you're married to, Sabina. I have a witness, Johns, in the town gaol at this moment; he'll be telling his story to the sheriff soon as he gets back from Blue Rocks.'

'It's a lie!' Sabina attacked Flint with her bare hands, trying to get at his face.

Flint held her off.

'It's true, Sabina. After Johns talks to the law, nothing can save Berry – you'd best accept that.'

Sabina stood glaring at him, trembling in fury.

'Reece couldn't . . . it's not true!' she said savagely. 'You're making it up, out of spite.'

Flint went on: 'Berry doesn't love yuh, Sabina – he never has. All he wants is control of Horseshoe, and he's using you to get that. He killed your father for that end. That's why he married you.

125

Don't yuh see the danger you're in? He intends to get rid of you, too, then Horseshoe will be his . . .' Sabina threw back her head and laughed hysterically.

'I see it all now,' she cried out. 'You're jealous – jealous because you wanted to marry me. Reece loves me – loves me, d'you hear? Now – get out!'

Flint looked unhappily at her. This scene was not what he had planned at all. He waited for her to calm down before speaking again.

'Sabina,' he said gently, 'you must take me seriously. What I have told you is the truth. In remaining here, you are in danger of your life – Berry intends to kill you to get possession of the Horseshoe.'

She was like a wildcat, spitting fury.

'Fool!' she raged. 'You stupid fool! Reece loves me – of course he won't harm me. He never killed my father – never!'

She whirled across the room, pulling out a drawer of the desk so violently that the contents scattered on the floor. She dropped to her knees, grabbing a revolver and pushing shells into the chamber. Flint jumped up and tore the gun from her hand. She fought him, using her long nails on his face. Her gypsy blood was up, her dark skin suffused with anger.

'Get out,' she hissed. 'Leave me alone. I'll set Reece to kill you for this . . .'

Flint said, helplessly: 'I can't leave you here

126

now. You must come away with me. Try to believe that I only want to help you.'

'I don't want your help,' Sabina stormed. She attacked him again. 'Get out – get off my land, d'you hear?'

Flint saw it was useless. She was too infatuated with Berry to see reason. He moved for the door, paused, and called back:

'If you need me, I'll be at the Lazy S. Don't take any chances with Berry.'

He went out to the patio and mounted his horse. Sabina ran to the door, shouting abuse after him. Flint rode away.

He headed for Rimrock, bypassing the Lazy S ranch; there was Johns to be considered, and the sheriff, who might be back by now. Flint worried over leaving Sabina at the Horseshoe, but he comforted himself by thinking she would calm down soon; then she would realize the truth and break with Berry. He could do nothing till she helped herself. He had warned her, the rest was up to her.

The moon was full, a bright disc in the night sky. He kept away from the river and the cattle, and saw no one on the ride back. There were plenty of lights on Rimrock's Main Street, and a bustle of people. A hubbub of noise rose in the air, an excitement in front of the town gaol. Something had happened since Flint had ridden to the Horseshoe.

He forced his way through the crowd, to the steps of the gaol. There he saw Nora, with Dan Hurst and Kincaid. Nora came running towards him.

'It's Johns,' she said. 'He's been shot dead!'

Flint cursed. The witness he had relied on to convict Berry would be unable to speak.

'Did anyone see it?' he asked tensely. 'Who did the shooting?'

Nora's father answered. 'No one saw it, Matt. We heard gunshots and came to investigate. Johns was still locked in the cell, lying on his back – he'd been murdered in cold blood.'

A man in the crowd volunteered: 'I saw a man riding off, going at a mad pace. Couldn't see his face though, and it was too dark to pick up his trail.'

Berry, Flint thought bitterly; it must have been Berry – no one else would want Johns dead. Somehow, he had learnt that Flint had gaoled the gambler, and was holding him ready to talk to the sheriff, he had murdered him to protect himself.

'He was shot from the window,' Kincaid said. 'We haven't been able to get to him yet. You got the key, Matt?'

Flint nodded dully. He still had the key of the cell in his pocket. He went inside and unlocked the door. Johns lay sprawled on the floor, his shirt matted with blood. He was quite dead.

'Shot three times in the chest, without a chance

128

to defend himself,' Dan Hurst grunted. 'That ain't a human way to kill a man. Damn it, Matt; we've got to stop this business before there's any more killing.'

They laid out the body of Johns on a bunk and covered it over with a blanket, then went outside.

Flint said: 'Arnold back yet?'

Kincaid answered: 'We heard he's in the neighbourhood, with the county marshal. They're out looking at the river, and the cattle. That's why we rode into town. They ain't showed up yet.'

Nora looked searchingly at Flint, and asked: 'Did you see Sabina?'

'Yes; she wouldn't believe me. She still thinks Berry is in love with her.'

Kincaid's hands clenched, and he swore softly. 'If anything happens to her . . .'

Flint was badly worried. Berry had murdered Johns to stop him talking – and now Sabina knew the truth, even if she didn't believe it. If she mentioned his visit to Berry . . . he sweated over the thought, really alarmed for her.

'We've got to pick up Berry, before he reaches Sabina,' he asserted. 'Tonight – there's no time to waste. She's in danger.'

'I'll come with you,' Kincaid said. Nora bit her lip.

'It's always Sabina who comes between us, Matt,' she said in a low voice. 'Are you sure it's me you love?'

129

'Nora-'

But she was gone, running through the crowd, away from him. Flint started after her, half-angry, but horsemen riding into town cut him off. He halted, looking up at the newcomers. Arnold was in the lead, with a man he had never seen before; and there was Buchan with Bill Yates, and Inigo Webb.

Arnold called to him: 'Matt, this is Ned Payne, county marshal from Blue Rocks. He's taking charge here.'

Flint looked at Payne and liked the man. The marshal had the bearing of a veteran, with a weather-seamed face and keen eyes. He had a lean, spare frame, and a long moustache.

'Glad you're here, Marshal,' Flint said. 'There's been two more killings since the sheriff left, and things are about ready to blow up.'

Ned Payne dismounted. He wore black trousers and coat with two guns; his white shirt had a stiff collar and a black ribbon tie. His law badge was a large glittering star, prominently displayed. No man was going to take the marshal for other than he was; a lawman with a strong sense of duty.

'We'll talk in your office, Arnold,' the marshal said. 'I want you to join us, Flint. The rest of yuh wait outside.'

Payne had a brisk, decisive manner, and no one argued with him. They went into the sheriff's office, and Payne kicked the door shut. He took

Arnold's desk as if it were his own, placed his hat on the top, and lit a black cheroot.

'All right, Flint,' he said at once. 'Tell me everything that's happened.'

Matt Flint told him how he had tried to stop Berry blocking the gorge, of his being taken prisoner and escape; how Ben Storey had been shot down while trying to get his herd to water; how he had overheard the meeting between Berry and Johns, and how Johns had been shot while in prison.

Payne did not interrupt; he kept his eyes sternly on Flint's face and smoked his cheroot.

Flint finished: 'So you see how it is, Marshal. Sabina is in considerable danger, and we've got to move fast if we're to save her.'

Payne said: 'I'm not a man to waste time. I'd have been here earlier, except that I was out of town on a job. Arnold had to wait for me.'

Sheriff Arnold broke in: 'We've looked at the dried-up river and talked with Buchan and Webb. It sure is obvious the cattle have got to have water in the next few hours, or there won't be a herd left 'cepting Horseshoe's.'

Flint, looked at Payne challengingly. 'Well, Marshal,' he asked, 'what are you going to do?'

Ned Payne crushed out his cheroot and rose to his feet.

'You've done a good job,' he told Flint, 'and your word's good enough for me. I'm swearing in a posse, pronto, and riding out to Horseshoe. I'm bringing in Reece Berry on a charge of murder. And we'll take dynamite and open up Rimrock Creek – that may not be strictly legal, but I hate to see good cattle dying for nothing, I'm prepared to take full responsibility for my actions.'

Flint heaved a sigh of relief.

'That's good. Let's be moving while we've the moon to help us.'

Payne said: 'Wait. I'll rely on you to pick the men for this trip. About a dozen. And I don't want *hombres* who'll go off half-cocked, shooting at anything. This is a law posse, and the men in it will take my orders.'

Sheriff Arnold unlocked a cupboard and brought out a rifle and box of shells. Loading the gun, he said:

'There's me and you, Payne. Flint and Dan Hurst. That's four. Kincaid makes five-'

Matt Flint grinned.

'I'll pick the others,' he said. 'Leave it to me.' He went to the door and opened it. 'Kincaid – round up every ex-Horseshoe rider in town. All the men who worked under me for Piers Lomax. We've one last job to do for the old man!'

Kincaid disappeared in the crowd. Matt Flint hurried to the stables to get himself another horse; he'd already ridden his roan hard that night, and felt the need for a fresh mount. Dan Hurst brought dynamite from the store.

132

When the posse was formed, Marshal Ned Payne swore in every man as his deputy, and they rode out of town. Each man had his silent thoughts, but in one respect, they thought alike. Lomax's Horseshoe range was going to be cleaned up. Reece Berry and his hired gunmen had reached the end of their time.

Under a bright moon, the posse rode to the showdown.

12

A WOMAN'S FURY

Sabina was alone, awaiting the return of her husband. She paced the long, spacious living room of the Horseshoe ranchhouse, staring through the window from time to time, then continuing her pacing. It was an hour since Flint had left her, and, in that time, she had calmed herself.

Doubts crept into her mind. She loved Reece; she told herself that over and over again. And he loved her. But he wasn't the man she had thought him before they married – she had to admit that. In some ways, he disappointed her, even shocked her.

He could be brutal, cold-blooded, a man who dispensed death as if that action meant nothing to him. But still, she loved him . . . or did she? There were times when she doubted even that. If he had murdered her father. . . .

134

She stopped the thought before it went any further. She would face him with Flint's accusation when he returned, and learn the truth. She had to know. She needed Berry to put his arms about her once more, to whisper his love for her and deny this terrible thing.

The gun lay on the table, where Flint had tossed it, and, on impulse, she picked it up and loaded it, then thrust it into the pocket of her riding skirt. She was not good at waiting. The minutes dragged out and her doubts became increased torment.

From the window, she could see the lone pine and the wooden cross marking her father's grave. Her face clouded in sombre thought; the life she had led recently would have earned his severe disapproval. It was all Reece's fault, she thought savagely, everything she had done had been for him.

She knew her own nature well, wild and impetuous, but she was not bad. Then how had she got into this mess? Had she changed in some subtle way? She was not pleased with the things she had done – there was Luke Parrish's death and the way she had tried to buy her way clear with the bag of gold. Conscience money! Firing men who had been loyal to her father for many years – on Reece's word alone. And she didn't like the new men he had hired in their place.

There was Flint, too. Though she had never got

n well with him, she had always respected him as her father's foreman. She didn't like to think of the madness that had come over her when she ordered him to be tortured. Suppose he was right about her husband. . . .

Had she lain in the arms of her father's murderer and given him her kisses? The thought was needle-sharp agony stabbing at her brain . . . oh, Reece, Reece, you can't have done this thing!

Ben Storey had been shot, too. She'd never liked Storey, but murder was a word she shrank from. The threat of range war had long since passed; she had nothing to fear from the small ranchers now. Then why didn't she put a stop to the new tyranny that Horseshoe was inflicting on men like Dan Hurst? With the river diverted from its natural course, thousands of cattle were in danger of dying from thirst – and she was a cattle-man's daughter. It spelt ruin for scores of families who had built their lives about Rimrock.

She had set herself above the law because of Reece. He wanted power, unlimited power, she sensed that. He would never be content until he had every man in the district under his thumb. And yet she loved him. If he loved her, she had no regret for the course she had taken – but did he? Or was Flint right? Was it only the Horseshoe that Reece wanted? Was he using her simply to gain power?

There was the taste of ashes in her mouth. If he

had murdered her father to get at her, she would hate him as no other woman had ever hated before. She would take her revenge. . . .

The sound of horses came from the patio. She ran to the door and opened it wide. Reece was there, dismounting and hitching his horse to the rail. Calhoun and others of the new Horseshoe crew were with him.

Sabina looked at them; rough men with the killer stamp plain in their faces, men who were never without guns. She felt revulsion. What had she in common with such men? They had no place on her range.

Berry and Calhoun came towards the house; the others went into the punchers' cabin. There was something different now about Reece Berry, Sabina saw; the languid pose that he usually assumed had gone – in its place was a cold taut-ness. His handsome face looked harder, his slim, smartly-dressed body was tense as a stretched rope.

He saw her waiting, read her face, and called:

'Anything wrong, Sabina?'

His smile was forced.

She said: 'I must talk to you, Reece – alone.' She looked contemptuously at Calhoun as she spoke, then added: 'Matt Flint was here.'

Berry's dark eyes glittered.

'The devil he was,' he said softly, and exchanged a glance with the ugly man. 'Wait outside, Cal.'

He followed Sabina into the living room and closed the door.

'What's this about, Sabina?' he asked sharply. 'What did Flint want?'

She studied his face before replying, and saw nothing there to quiet her fears. She burst out:

'Reece – do you love me?'

He laughed. 'Of course I do, darling.' He took a step towards her, to caress her.

Sabina moved back, keeping her gaze on his face.

'Really and truly love me, Reece?'

Annoyance showed in his eyes. He stood watching her, took a cigarette from his pocket, placed it between his lips and lit it. The smoke curled upwards.

'What did Flint tell you?' he demanded.

Sabina thrust her right hand into the pocket of her riding skirt; her fingers crept round the butt of the gun she had there. The moment wasn't quite real for her; almost, she felt hysterical. She couldn't be accusing her husband like this. . . .

She seemed to hear her own words as if they were spoken by someone else.

'Flint said that you killed my father, that he has a man called Johns ready to bear witness against you.'

Reece Berry laughed harshly.

'Johns won't do any talking. He-'

He stopped suddenly, realizing his mistake. He

138

had said the wrong thing, and now Sabina knew. He could read it in her face, the first stunned look of shock, then the swiftly-rising fury.

'It's true,' she cried, 'true! Oh God, what have I done!'

Still Berry wasn't seriously alarmed. He had about finished with her anyway and was ready to get rid of her.

He jeered: 'Sure it's true. I never loved yuh. I just wanted-'

His words died away as Sabina's hand came from her pocket. She had a gun, pointed at him. Cursing, Berry's hands dropped to his gunbelt. He wasn't fast enough. Sabina fired, and the shot sounded like a violent explosion in the room.

The cigarette fell from Berry's lips as he shrieked in agony. The shell hit his knee-cap, smashing the bone. He staggered still screaming, and lost his balance as his leg gave way. He hit the floor, writhing in pain and holding his knee.

Sabina stood over him, her face white and fixed in horror. It was as if she wore a mask.

She pointed the gun down at him, and said:

'You're the foulest thing I've ever known – you're not a man at all! You murdered my father and pretended to love me. I'm going to kill you, Reece. I'm going to-'

She never finished. The shot had been heard. The door crashed open and Calhoun came into the room like an angry bear. He flung himself upon her, knocking the gun from her hand, his weight carrying her across the room. Sabina's head hit the wall and she slid to the floor, unconscious.

Berry stopped screaming. He began to swear, gritted hia teeth and drew his gun.

'Stand aside, Calhoun,' he shouted. 'She's crippled me – I'm going to finish her now!'

He rolled over and took aim.

Calhoun said: 'Don't be a fool, Reece. You can't shoot a woman and get away with it. It's got to look like an accident.'

'Get out of the way, you fool!'

Berry was almost fainting with pain, not knowing what he did. Calhoun didn't want any part of it. He left the fallen figure of the girl and moved quickly to Berry. Cursing, he wrenched the gun from his hand.

'Not that way, Reece. It must be another accident, like Lomax. Do you want to throw away everything you've planned for?'

Berry supported his body on his elbows, glaring at Sabina. Sweat ran down his face and his mouth worked with the pain of his shattered knee. He shook his head, to clear it, cunning returning.

'All right, Cal – I'll wait. Now get Slim to fix my leg.'

The ugly man went to the door and shouted for Slim, the only one of Berry's gang who had any knowledge of medicine. Slim came, cut away Berry's trouser leg and inspected the wound. He shook his head. 'Nasty mess, Reece. I can patch it up so yuh can be moved, but you'll want the doc to work on this.' Calhoun lifted Sabina's unconscious form and placed her in a chair; he tied her hands behind her back, then watched Slim at work.

Slim used hot water and a sponge to wash away the blood and loose fragments of bone, dosing Berry liberally with whisky to deaden the pain. Then he strapped a wooden splint in place, and bandaged it.

'No more I can do,' he said. 'Better send a man for the doc right away. Longer yuh wait, the less the chance there is of saving your leg.'

Reece Berry cursed savagely.

'Damn the bitch – she'll pay for this! I'll make her sweat before she dies. And Flint – if it hadn't been for him, I'd have caught her unawares.' His eyes glowed with the killer light.

'I'll stake him down and raw-hide the skin off his back, and leave him in the desert to die of thirst!'

He lit a cigarette, puffed furiously at it, his teeth shredding the end.

'For God's sake give me the whisky bottle again – my knee feels like hell. . . .

Sabina stirred in the chair. She opened her eyes and sat up, her arms straining at the ropes. For a moment her face was blank, then she saw Berry and her eyes blazed with fury. Realization of the mistake she'd made had been a long time coming,

141

but now that she knew how she had been duped, a bitter loathing swamped her. She struggled to her feet, hissing:

'You never loved me at all. You murdered my father in cold blood and-'

'Shut up,' Calhoun said, and pushed her back into the chair.

'You'll hang,' Sabina spat at Berry. 'You'll hang for your foul crimes. Matt Flint will get you in the end!'

Slim came back to report that he'd dispatched a man to Rimrock for the doctor.

Sabina laughed bitterly. 'I hope your leg festers and drops off. I hope your whole body rots away. I hope-'

Calhoun slammed his fist into her mouth and snarled: 'Quit that stuff!'

Berry grinned maliciously.

'Flint hasn't got anything on me. Johns is dead – I killed him myself, to make sure he wouldn't talk. And soon, you're going to die, leaving me the Horseshoe range, as I planned from the beginning. Like your father, you're going to have an accident.'

He lifted himself, shouted: 'Cal, get me a stick to lean on. Slim, saddle four horses, pronto – we've time to get rid of her before the doc arrives.'

Slim looked doubtful.

'You're in no condition for riding,' he objected. 'You ought to rest up and-'

'Get the horses, damn yuh!' Berry raged. He was half-mad with pain, half-drunk from the whiskey. 'She did this to me, and I'm going to see she pays for it.'

Slim went out. Berry stood up, leaning heavily on the stick Calhoun handed him. Sweat poured off his face and he gritted his teeth. He began to swear under his breath.

'You smashed my leg,' he snarled at Sabina, 'but that's nothing to what I'm going to do to you! I'm taking yuh up to Rimrock Creek and I'm going to push you off the top. Then I'm going to dynamite the cliff face and bury yuh under tons of rock – I reckon that'll look enough like an accident!'

Sabina Lomax looked at her husband and shuddered.

'Flint will get you,' she said.

Berry threw the empty whisky bottle at her.

'Flint!' he snapped. 'Always it's Flint who spoils things – but he won't save you, Sabina. Nothing can save you! And I'll deal with Flint before long.'

Calhoun carried Sabina outside and tied her on a horse. Slim helped Berry into the saddle, and the four of them rode away from the ranch.

'Take a last look,' Reece Berry jeered. 'Yuh won't be seeing it again, Sabina. From now on, Horseshoe is mine!'

There was bright moonlight and the grave under the lone pine stood out stark and clear. A lump formed in Sabina's throat. Her father lay there, murdered by the man at her side, the man to whom she had been a wife. She was calmer now; the hatred was still there, but tempered with regret. What a fool she had been! If only she'd listened to Matt Flint. . . .

They rode slowly because Berry's leg was a burning agony. Across the cattle plain they went, into the foothills, climbing towards Rimrock Creek. Sabina kept silent. Words were no use now. She had no hope for her own life, only a quiet certainty that Berry would not live to enjoy the wealth of Horseshoe. Flint would see to that.

Sand and cactus and rock began to appear in the moonlight. The slope steepened and their progress slowed to a crawl. Higher and higher they climbed, between gaunt pines and bare rock, the river a broad silver strip far below.

Calhoun reined in his horse, holding his head to one side, listening.

'Thought I heard gunshots,' he said. 'Yeah, there it is again.'

Berry laughed.

'Only one of the ranchers trying to get his herd to water. Nothing to worry us. Get on!'

They rode on up the narrow trail, slower now, measuring their pace to Berry's. He sat his horse, white and sweating, his leg burning like a furnace. He rocked in the saddle, becoming delirious. Only his mad desire to kill Sabina with his own hands kept him going at all.

The sound of hoofs on the trail behind became louder. Calhoun swore, turning his horse and drawing his gun. Four men were coming after them, driving their mounts hard.

'It's Pete and the others,' he said. 'Something must have gone wrong.'

Berry waited impatiently for his riders to catch up. When they did, the leader cried out:

'Flint's after us with a posse headed by Marshal Payne. The game's up, Reece! We've got to run for it.'

Berry slid awkwardly out of the saddle, pulling his gun clear of its holster.

'We'll make our stand here,' he said coldly. 'But first, Sabina must die!'

13

GUNS AT
RIMROCK CREEK

The posse reached the river bank, rode down the slope and splashed noisily through the water. From the other side, a voice hailed them:

'You *hombres* had better turn back unless yuh want trouble.' Flint recognized the voice of one of the few Horseshoe men left who had worked for Piers Lomax.

He shouted back: 'This is a law posse under Marshal Payne. We want Reece Berry for murder.' There was silence. Flint and Ned Payne rode up to the man on patrol, and the marshal said crisply:

'Where's Berry?'

The sight of Payne's silver star combined with the body of riders backing him was enough to ensure cooperation from a man who had never liked Berry's handling of the Horseshoe.

146

'He rode back to the ranch-house a while back,' came the instant reply. 'He wasn't alone – better watch out for gunplay if you're aiming to take him in.'

Kincaid said, anxiously: 'Is Sabina at the ranch?'

The rider shrugged his shoulders. 'So far as I know.'

The posse rode on, crossing the rolling plain to Horseshoe ranch in bright moonlight. Far away to their right, the herd made a dark mass against the silhouette of the mountains.

A rider came along the trail, towards Rimrock. Seeing the posse, he turned abruptly and galloped back. Sheriff Arnold cursed.

'He's going to warn Berry,' he said.

Payne didn't appear worried.

'We'll bc right on his heels,' the marshal drawled. 'Let him go.'

They covered the remaining miles at a swift pace. Ahead, the ground sloped gently down to the clustered buildings of the Horseshoe spread. The man who had turned back rode into the patio, firing off his gun to give the alarm. He slid from his mount, running for the house and shouting.

Men came out from lighted doorways, guns in their hands, as the posse arrived. Payne held his men back, advancing alone.

'I'm arresting Reece Berry for murder,' he called out. 'You other *hombres* had better stay clear unless yuh mean to join him on the lynchtree!'

For answer, he received a volley of lead. He dropped from his horse, took cover in the shadow of a barn, and waved on Flint and the others.

'Surround the house and take Berry,' he ordered.

The Horseshoe gunmen had scattered, ducking behind barrels and outhouses. A brisk exchange of gunfire ensued as both parties settled to the fight. In the rear, Flint and Kincaid looked at each other.

Kincaid said: 'Sabina will be in the house,' and Flint nodded. They moved together, running from cover to cover, making for the rear of the house. Lead whined past their heads, but they did not turn back. The last few yards had to be crossed in moonlight; heads down, they ran over open ground, gunshots echoing and bullets kicking up the dust about them. They reached the shadow of the house and flattened out against the wooden wall of the building.

Flint smashed a window with his gun and climbed through. A man came running, making a dark form in the doorway. Flint threw up his gun and fired. Red flame stabbed through the room; the shot crashed loudly and the man groaned as the slug tore at his flesh.

Flint got to him fast, drove the gun from his hand and forced him into a corner. Kincaid

148

rammed his long Colt into the man's belly and bawled:

'Where's Sabina? Talk fast or I'll spill yore guts on the floor!' The gunman winced with pain.

'Go to hell!' he snarled.

Kincaid lifted his Colt and pistol-whipped the man's face.

'Where's Sabina, you rat?'

The gunman covered his face with his hands and sobbed. 'Berry's taken her up to Rimrock Creek. She shot him through the knee and crippled him-'

Kincaid swore, and brought down his gun on the man's head, stunning him. Flint thought how Berry would be feeling; a smashed knee-cap was one of the most painful wounds a man could suffer; he would be driven nearly crazy, desperate enough for anything.

'We've got to hurry,' he said, and ran through the house to the front porch.

Outside, the noise of gunfire had slackened. The sound of hoofbeats came, and Arnold's voice:

'They're getting away!'

Then Ned Payne was standing in the open, a gun in each hand and a cheroot clamped between his teeth; the silver star was bright on his chest.

'You, Flint, seen anything of Berry?' he demanded. Flint vaulted into the saddle of his horse, calling back:

'Berry's taken the girl up to Rimrock Creek.'

He rode off, with Kincaid on his heels and the posse forming up again. Ahead, the gunmen were driving their mounts hard for the foothills leading into the mountains; Rimrock Creek was up there, and Reece Berry with Sabina.

Flint used his spurs to get the utmost from his horse, riding madly. Kincaid's face was pale and drawn, a grim mask. Both then knew they might well be too late to help Sabina – and both were determined to spare no effort to save her.

The chase stretched out, Berry's gunmen in the lead, closely followed by Flint and Kincaid, with Payne and the rest of the posse coming up behind. They reached the end of the grassland, swept on through rising foothills to the trail that led up to Rimrock Creek. The mountains were ghost-pale in the moonlight, the pines stark and bare. The narrow path ran like a ribbon up to the gorge and the heights above the river.

Flint was sweating; he could guess why Berry had brought the girl up here . . . The night air grew steadily cooler and the wind became a whiplash on his face. Higher they climbed, towards the plateau where Flint had put up his fight to prevent the gorge being dynamited.

Kincaid shouted: 'There they are – Berry and Sabina!'

Flint saw that the men they had been chasing had dismounted and were scattering to the cover of rocks. Berry had a gun in his hand as he

150

hobbled to shelter. Two men dragged Sabina over the rocks.

Kincaid started firing too soon, warning Berry of their approach. Rifles cracked, further up the trail, and Kincaid's horse threw up its forelegs and whinnied. Kincaid came out of the saddle and ran forward on foot, dodging from rock to rock, his gun crashing flame and lead.

'Leave her alone, Berry,' he shouted. 'Harm her and I swear you'll die so slow you'll go screaming into hell!'

Reece Berry laughed wildly and began shooting. Lead hummed through the air and ricocheted off rocks. The night was noisy with gunshots, bright with crimson flashes. Flint caught up with Kincaid and hauled the tall puncher to shelter.

'You won't help her by getting yourself shot to pieces,' he said. 'Keep your head down and wait. Payne's right behind and we need more men before we can rush them.'

Kincaid grunted and shot back at the gunmen higher up the path. He snaked forward on his belly, swearing as a shot lifted his hat. Flint dug himself in, covering Kincaid with his fire. Berry's men had the advantage of position and he didn't see how they were going to shift them.

Behind him, the posse arrived, springing from the saddle and rushing to join the fight. Payne's voice sounded over the firing:

'This is the law, Berry. I call on yuh to throw

down yore gun and give yourself up.'

Berry jeered: 'Come and get me, Marshal,' and emptied his gun at the lawman.

Payne dropped flat, shouting fresh orders.

'All right, men, he's had his chance – now move in and take him. Keep your bullets away from the girl.'

He broke into a run, moving from rock to rock, creeping up on Berry's position. It seemed to Flint that he was in a crossfire; with slugs ricocheting in every direction, all he could do was hug the ground. Kincaid was somewhere ahead of him.

Ned Payne joined him behind the boulder, and both men reloaded.

Payne grunted: 'Cramps our style, Berry holding the girl. Can't afford to take chances.'

Flint caught sight of Berry and fired. His shot missed and a fusillade of lead came winging back. One of the posse groaned and rolled sideways. Kincaid darted forward again, risking his life to get to Sabina.

Payne's gun barked, giving him covering fire.

'He sure must love that gal,' the marshal drawled.

The shooting abated for a time, then Flint saw Sabina. Berry had her poised on the edge of the cliff, ready to push her over. Kincaid sprang forward, shouting wildly; a slug caught him and laid him low. He crawled forward desperately. . . .

Berry's mocking laughter echoed down the

mountainside. 'Yuh can't save her,' he jeered. 'None of yuh can save her now!'

Marshal Payne leapt into the open.

'Berry,' he called. 'Turn the girl free and I'll give yuh an hour's start. You've my word on it.'

'Too late, Marshal,' Berry said, and pushed Sabina into space. Flint's blood froze and he stared, helpless to do anything; the short hairs on his neck rose. He cursed Berry savagely – and the lead flew again.

Sabina disappeared over the edge of the cliff, screaming. Every man of the posse ran forward, maddened beyond caution by such a cold-blooded action. Ignoring the barrage of lead that Berry's men loosed on them, they rushed in with guns blazing. Sabina's scream stopped abruptly; so abruptly, that Flint crawled to the edge of the drop and looked down.

The stump of a tree had broken her fall, some twenty feet below. She hung in space, her feet scraping the rock wall. She was alive, but half-stunned; and any move might send her to her death.

Flint ran back along the trail, snatched the lariat from his saddle and cast the noose for the tree stump. He circled it first throw, tightened it and tested it. It should hold. He swung himself over the edge and landed with bruising force against the cliff, below the stump.

'Hold on, Sabina,' he called. 'Hold on till I reach yuh.'

153

Above him, the gunfire broke out with renewed fury. Berry was making his last stand. Sabina did not move. She lay limp, her shirt torn and her black hair hanging down. Moonlight showed a ledge some distance below, a narrow outcrop from the rock face. He had to get her down to that – there was no other way.

Flint went up the rope, hand over hand, reached Sabina and felt her gently. She seemed to have no broken bones. She was barely conscious, whimpering with fright, and clung to him tightly, crying over and over:

'Matt! Take me home, Matt – take me home-'

Flint got her clear of the stump and held her with one arm while he slid down the rope. He was sweating freely, his arms aching from the strain. It seemed he would never reach safety – then his boots scraped the ledge and he could stand again. He took a moment, getting his breath, then inched along the narrow ledge, towards the slope of the cliff.

A pair of hands reached out to help him and Flint looked up at Dan Hurst.

'Let me have her, Matt,' the rancher said.

Between them, they hauled Sabina to safety and laid her on the ground. Flint stood up, reaching for his guns.

'There's still Berry to settle with,' he said grimly, and went up the trail again.

It was almost over. Before the angry rush of the

posse, Berry's men broke and ran for it, deserting their boss. They sprang to saddle and rode off into the mountains. Reece Berry lay on the ground, his broken leg preventing his escape with them. He lay there, his guns empty, waiting for the posse to take him.

Only Kincaid reached him first. . . .

The tall puncher was wounded, crawling over the ground. He had seen Berry push Sabina over the cliff, but hadn't seen Flint save her. He thought she was dead, murdered by Berry, and there was no mercy in him, only the burning desire for vengeance.

Berry saw him coming, saw the gun slowly, swing to blast him to eternity – and began to scream for mercy. Kincaid's eyes were blue ice-chips. His finger tightened on the trigger. Reece Berry forgot his injured leg and tried to stand upright; he was near the edge of the cliff, swaying unsteadily.

Kincaid fired, and the slug took Berry low down, driving him backwards. Berry's one good leg slipped on the brink; he lost his balance and leant into space. His arms waved wildly, uselessly. He fell, screaming, over the mountainside. . . .

His scream slowly died away as he fell to his death on the floor of the canyon, a hundred feet below. He died the way he had intended to kill his wife, and no one in the posse wasted a second's pity on him.

Flint reached Kincaid and bent to inspect his wounds. He had a slug in his leg and another in his shoulder; neither wound was serious, though they had left him weak. He'd be on his feet again in a few days.

Kincaid murmured: 'I got him, Matt. I got him – for Sabina!'

Flint smiled gently.

'Sabina's safe. A tree stump broke her fall and we just got her up from the cliff. You'll be seeing her soon.'

Kincaid said nothing, but from the way his face lit up Flint knew what he was thinking – and, suddenly, he wanted to get back and see Nora. Only one of Berry's men lay on the plateau; Calhoun, with a bullet hole between his eyes. The ugly man had paid for Luke Parrish's death. The posse rode back to Rimrock.

Payne did not chase the last of Berry's outfit; the marshal reckoned they would not be showing their faces around Rimrock again, and there were more important things to attend to. Cattle always come first to a cattleman – and the herds were dying for lack of water.

It was a very much subdued Sabina who came down from the mountains. The wildness had gone, and with it, all desire to rule the ranges. She threw open the Horseshoe spread to all the ranchers, inviting them to water their cattle on her land

156

until the gorge was cleared.

It took several days of dynamiting to undo what Reece Berry had done in a few minutes, but, finally, Rimrock Creek was clear again, and the river flowed along its natural course once more. Peace came to the ranges and life returned to normal.

Matthew Flint was sprucing himself up in Rimrock's hotel, ready to call on Nora Hurst when Sabina came to him. They looked at each other, and again there was that awkwardness between them. Sabina took the plunge.

'I've had my lesson, Matt, and learned from it. You were right and I wrong. I hope you'll come back to Horseshoe, as foreman . . . or . . . or in the way Dad would want it. You know how he felt about us.'

Flint saw the pleading in her eyes and felt uncomfortable. He said quietly:

'You haven't learned it all yet, Sabina. I love Nora, and I'm going to ask her to marry me.'

Sabina's eyes dropped.

'I thought-' she said, and stopped. 'Matt, you've done a lot to help me, even risked your life. Does that mean nothing?'

'It means I've tried to keep a promise I made your father. We couldn't make marriage work, Sabina – we just don't suit each other. Kincaid, now, he nearly got himself killed trying to save you. I figure he's going to be calling on yuh soon

157

as he gets around. He's a fine man, and would make a good foreman.'

Sabina said, 'Kincaid,' as if she'd never known a man of that name. She thought about it, and Flint could tell from the way her expression changed that she liked what she thought about it. She held out her hand, smiling.

'We'll shake on that, Matt. You're still teaching me things about myself. I'll be waiting when Kincaid shows up – and I wish you and Nora luck.'

Flint took her hand firmly.

'I reckon your Dad would be proud of yuh now,' he said.

She threw back her head, eyes gleaming.

'I'll try to keep that way, always.' She went through the door. 'You and Nora must call on us sometime, Matt.'

It was the emphasis she placed on the word 'us' that told Flint things were going to be all right at the Horseshoe. Whistling, he went to saddle his horse for the ride to the Lazy S.

Nora would be waiting – and it was time he spoke his piece.

C AB